Valerie

A Love Story

by

Anna Leigh

Copyright © 2019 Thomas Weaver LLC

All Rights Reserved

ISBN 13: 978-1-7321991-8-7

ISBN: 1-7321991-8-3

Dedication

To Barbara, Dale, and Christine – my life is so much richer because of you. I cannot imagine how much poorer my life would be without you. To Dale and Rita Weaver, who raised me. To John, Roland, Mark, and Gail, my brothers and sister – intrinsic to my life.

This book is a work of fiction. Names, characters, places, and incidents are the product of the author's imagination or are used fictitiously. Any resemblance to actual events or persons, living or dead is coincidental.

The scanning, uploading, and distribution of this work without permission is a theft of the author's intellectual property. Permission for use (other than review) may be obtained from TWeaver2008@aol.com

ALL RIGHTS RESERVED

T. Weaver

© Copyright 2019 by Thomas Weaver, LLC

ACKNOWLEDGEMENTS

This is my first attempt at a novel. It has not been edited professionally for many reasons. The story was finished in ten days. It isn't perfect. I'm sure my editor would suggest many changes. However, it is complete and among the things I've written, it makes me happiest – well, there is one other. It started out to be a different book completely, but the characters wouldn't allow that book to happen. They 'told' me how the story would go. I've heard authors say that, but didn't really believe it until it happened to me. So, my thanks to both Valerie and Jim.

Thanks to all of you who encouraged me and gave me the idea that I could actually finish a book. Thanks to all who gave me the experiences and knowledge that helped me craft a story.

Anna Leigh

Valerie – A Love Story

Halfway along the journey of our life,

Having strayed from the right path and lost it,

I awoke to find myself in a dark wood.

Dante Alighieri

The Divine Comedy – Hell

Canto 1

Of all the sad words of tongue or pen, the saddest are these, "It might have been."

John Greenleaf Whittier

Anna Leigh

One

Valerie rolled under her covers to glance at the window. The blinds were drawn, but she could tell from the dim light coming in that it was a cloudy day. Snow had been forecast, and she thought it might still be snowing. She knew it was cold. She could feel cold on her face, the only part of her body outside the layers of covers she was under.

She slowly peeled back the covers and sat on the bed. Even in her sweats and heavy socks, the room felt cold. Maybe it was the grayness, as well. Valerie slid her feet into white terry slippers, pulled a robe around herself, and padded across the carpeted floor to peek out the window.

There was a new coating of snow alright. She couldn't tell exactly how much, but she hoped it would be enough to close the school. She was dreading school. Her grades were excellent, that wasn't the problem. The problem was with the other students.

People. She had been invited to parties, but they involved the jocks - invited or not. She soon found that the jocks just liked to get the girls drunk, then naked. Sex usually followed. Many times, the jocks would make fun of the girls – in public – afterward. She was able to avoid the jocks – and parties after the first, and emerged with her virtue intact, but that only served to increase the hurtful things the jocks said, and it made her the object of many of the other girl's nasty comments, as well. She had half a year until graduation. She couldn't wait, even if she didn't quite know what was going to come after.

But, even if school was closed today, there would still be things to do. She was sure she would be shoveling the drive and sidewalks. Her mother wouldn't stoop to physical labor – for a woman who could play tennis with the best, somehow, she didn't have any strength when it came to menial tasks. And frankly, her father was useless.

"V-a-l-e-r-i-e!" It was her mom.

"Yes, mother."

"No school today." The words came from downstairs and were loud enough to be heard through Valerie's closed door. "It was on the news." There was a pause. "Still plenty to be done."

Valerie groaned.

"We need to get the drive and walk cleaned of snow." Her mother said it like 'we' were going to do it.

Valerie shed the robe she had worn over her sweats, shivering as she did so. She doffed the sweat pants and pulled on a pair of jeans. She shivered as she did this, too. She slid her sock feet into a pair of tennis shoes. She knew her clothes were inadequate, but she didn't have anything 'adequate' for work in the snow.

Stopping in the kitchen, she grabbed a piece of toast, then another before heading to the garage. The only shovel they had was a spade. Despite the fact that snow shovels weren't very expensive, her parents hadn't bothered to buy one. She had complained about it before only to be told by her father, "It doesn't snow often enough to buy a special shovel to do one job." Once before, she had responded that if he had to do the shoveling, he would probably think it was worth it. That got her grounded for a week.

As she stepped outside, she felt the cold through the thin jeans on her legs. She shivered and hoped that the work of shoveling the snow would help keep her warm. Valerie picked up the shovel, but the knitted mittens she'd donned made it hard to hold the handle. There was a slight breeze, and she felt herself getting colder already.

Two

I could tell from the light from the window that it was time to get up. But the bed was soft and warm, and the morning outside the bed was cold. I could almost feel the coldness of the hardwood floor from where I lay. It was January, and I guessed the forecast had been correct. At least six inches of new snow were expected since the storm started the night before.

I swung my legs out of the covers, and slipped my feet into the slippers at the side of the bed. Standing, I donned a terry robe and wrapped it around myself for warmth. A glance at the bed told me that my wife, Marsha, was still asleep. I descended the stairs and went into the kitchen. I made myself coffee. While it was brewing, I looked outside and saw there had indeed been six or seven inches of snow. It made the landscape pristine. I would have preferred to stay inside and not venture out, but the snow brought with it work to be done.

I live in suburbia. Nice houses. Manicured lawns. In the old days, people used to come out and talk to each other. In those days, homes were built with front porches, so you could say 'howdy' to passersby or invite the neighbors up for a drink and genteel conversation. I lived in such a place – once. Life seemed to move at a slower pace.

Not so much anymore. People move in and out. Neighbors stay inside their homes, or they work long hours and by the time they get home, they don't have much energy for socializing, even if they had the desire. Then again, even the socializing energy goes into schmoozing with those who can improve one's spot on the career ladder. And friends are relegated to Facebook, twitter (Let's stay connected in 140 characters.), and other sites where someone can broadcast meaningless drivel and think that it actually represents "keeping in touch."

I'm a consultant, of sorts. I do project management, and the jobs come and go. I do reasonably well financially, but I also have a fair amount of time to take care of things around the house: cleaning, laundry, lawn, etc. I structure my life that way. I'm relatively happy, and the homestead looks the way I want it to look. It is a little bit of control in a world that is chaotic.

I shaved and dressed – flannel-lined jeans and a sweater, then poured what was left of my coffee into an insulated cup. Before exiting the house into the garage, I put on my thick winter jacket and brown leather work boots. The boots were stiff and cold.

If the house was cold, the garage was frigid. I punched the button, and the garage door clattered open. Snow was still falling lightly. The neighborhood was quiet, the way snowfall has of quieting places. And then, too, other people were also reluctant to head outside. There was an excuse to stay inside in the warmth and comfort a little longer on a morning like this. I was about to shatter the calm of the morning with my snow-removing machine.

I'd grown up in cold country. I breathed in through my nose and felt the hairs stiffen; a sure sign that it was well below freezing. I moved to the back of the garage and threw back a tarp, revealing a snow blower. I had decided to buy one after a particularly heavy snow last year. Shoveling that stuff just about did me in – even if I was in decent physical shape. And, my back hurt for days. So, I'd purchased a snow blower – battery powered. That way, I didn't have to store gasoline in the garage, and I didn't have a cord to run over, either. If there was any other benefit, other than easier snow removal, it was that the machine was quieter than one powered by a gasoline engine.

I plugged in the battery and started it up. It did a pretty good job, and cut the time to clear the drive and sidewalk down to about ten minutes. An easy ten minutes, at that. I was just about done when I noticed the teenaged daughter who lived next door shoveling their drive with a spade – a shovel that was designed for digging holes, not for this job. She was wearing jeans, a blue ski jacket, tennis shoes, and knitted mittens. Except for the jacket, her clothing was inadequate to the task. Even the jeans – they were too tight to allow for insulating air. Her dark blond hair was tied in a ponytail. And the jeans, tight-fitting as they were, showed the shape of her legs. Not that many years ago, she was kind of a lanky little girl. If her legs were any indication, she was well on her way to being a shapely young woman. I shook my head to clear the thoughts.

I walked over to where she was working. "Hi. You're not going to get this cleared very fast with that thing," I said.

Valerie looked up to see him. He had a nice, friendly smile. "I know, but it is the best we have," she replied. "Dad says it only snows a couple of times a year, and it isn't worth buying a 'special' shovel for the job. But this thing is a pain." His hair was sand-colored. She knew that from seeing him working in his yard. His eyes were a pale blue. She hadn't seen his eyes before. She was glued to his eyes. There was something about them. They were twinkling, alive, and at the same time, soft and understanding.

"Mind if I help?" I asked. Her eyes were brown, and her skin was almost pale – except for the slight rosy glow on her cheeks. Her face was lovely, and the thoughts of her becoming a beautiful young woman returned before I could force them out and return to the task at hand.

"Do you have a better shovel?" she asked, looking up at his face a few inches above hers. His slightly tan face was clean shaven. Her dad didn't shave unless it was absolutely necessary. He was dressed for the cold. His jacket and trousers fit him well and while they were obviously work clothes, they were well cared for.

"Sort of," I said. "Better living through technology."

I walked back over and returned with the snow blower. I ran it back and forth over the drive, shifting the chute with each pass to make sure the snow was blown into their yard rather than on their, or my, cleaned drive. Then, I did the front and street sidewalk, as well. It took little effort and about ten minutes of my time.

"Thank you so very much," she said. "I would have been out here for hours. And my hands and feet were already cold. Well, freezing."

"You are more than welcome," I replied. "I'm glad I could help, and it wasn't much of an effort on my part."

"My name is Valerie," she said, and she held out her mittened hand for me to shake. She had an infectious smile. I took off my glove and shook her hand.

"And my name is Jim," I replied.

"I'm not sure my parents – especially my dad – would want me to tell them the man next door, 'Jim' helped with the drive. They are kind of fanatics about calling adults by their last names."

"Well. My name is still Jim, but you can tell them old Mr. Connor next door helped out with his snow blower."

Valerie giggled. "You're not old. But thank you, again. Can I help you put things away?" She wasn't in a hurry to get back into the house where she knew more chores awaited her. Besides, she decided that she wanted to spend a little more time with this man that she'd only seen at a distance until now.

"Well, there isn't much to do," I said, but thinking she wanted to tag along, "but you can help, if you like."

We took the snow blower back into the garage. I unplugged the battery and asked Valerie to put it into the charger, pointing out where it was. Then, I threw the tarp back over the machine.

"So, you are in high school, Valerie?"

"I'm a senior this year. Six more months after this, and I graduate. I'm not sure what I'll do then. I thought about college, but high school is such a pain, I don't know."

"College is different – a LOT different," I said. "Fewer classes. More free time, although more study time is needed. You get to pick what you want to study – at least a lot more. I hated high school. I very much liked college."

"Really?" she asked, "what did you study?"

"Science. Physics, chemistry, math."

"Is that what you do now?"

"Actually, not really. I have a business of my own. I work from home. I create and manage projects for my clients."

"What do you mean?" she asked.

"Well, suppose you want to open a restaurant. But you don't know how to do that. I talk to you and create a plan – the steps you need to take to get the job done: financing the restaurant, leasing the site, those sort of things – and places along the plan where you will check on your progress. In the Navy, we called it POA&M – plan of attack and milestones."

"Oh. I've got a school project, actually the last big project before graduation, and I don't know where to start. The teacher hasn't been any help, and my parents don't understand."

"What's the project?" I asked.

"I'm not even sure it is a 'real' project. Three of us have to put together a report on life in Medieval Europe. The report has to be twenty pages," she drew out the word twenty as if a judge had given her a twenty-year sentence. "Then, we have to give an oral report in front of the whole class."

"Okay," I said, "it sounds relatively simple from a planning view. You have to set a plan – determine what information you will need and where you are going to get it . . ."

"The internet isn't allowed," she interrupted.

"Well, a lot of sites on the internet are notoriously bad when it comes to information, but those sites might have references, and the references can give you a fair amount of information. You'll probably have to spend some time in the library. Actually, the university might be a good resource."

"But you'll need to decide what you want in your report. You might concentrate on day-to-day information, or what the government, if you can call it that, was; what happened when people got sick; all those aspects of life. You'll need to decide how long you have to write the paper, plan on at least two revisions, and if you want visuals for your class presentation. You have three people, so you can split up the work, although one of you will have to be a leader of sorts. And assignments will have to be made – who is responsible for what. Then, you should have meetings at least every week to make sure everything is on track."

"So, your first meeting should be about putting together a plan and dividing the work," I finished.

"I never thought of all that," she said. "Could I ask you for help?"

"Sure." I dug a business card out of my pocket. "Feel free to call or e-mail me, and I'll help you in any way I can."

About that time, we heard a female voice calling, "V-a-l-e-r-i-e," from next door.

"Time to go," she said. "I hope I'm not in trouble because I didn't do the drive with the crappy shovel we have."

Then, she was gone. I had to smile. When the weather was decent, Valerie would kick a soccer ball around her back yard. I didn't know if she was on a team, but I wondered about her skills. About twice a week, her ball would end up in our back yard. So, about twice a week, I'd pick it up and toss it back over the fence. I tried to kick it back one time, but if anything, I was much worse than she was at kicking a soccer ball.

I closed the garage door, after a minute, and reentered the house, depositing my work boots just inside the garage door.

"Flirting with the neighbor girl?" My wife had finally gotten out of bed. I'm not sure how many layers she had on. Her shape was indistinct under at least three robes and her pajamas. Big fleece boots completed the look.

"Sorry?"

"You were talking with the neighbor girl."

"Yes, her dad gave her a spade and wanted her to clear the drive with it. After I finished our drive and walk, I used the snow blower to help her out."

"And the spent time chatting. Mind if I ask what you were talking about?"

"Yes, we talked. About what I do, then I gave her a free consultation for a school project she is working on. And why do you care – apparently so much?"

"Just giving you a hard time. But we wouldn't want the neighbors to talk. It would be bad for business."

Yes, Lord knows, we wouldn't want to do anything that was bad for business. Who knows, Marsha, maybe she will buy a house from you. Then, you wouldn't be worried about the neighbors talking.

Marsha poured a cup of coffee and retired to the bedroom, where she would prepare herself for a day at the office, or elsewhere. She is a real estate agent – hard driving, always looking to get the next listing, or sale, and pursuing an upward career. She was on track to become a real estate tycoon. It was a track of her own making, and it had become an obsession. Right now, career is everything, and our relationship is a distant second. It wasn't always that way. Maybe I just thought it wasn't. She always tells me there will be plenty of time "later," after she has established herself as the queen of real property ("You'll be sooooo proud of me.") in our city. We didn't have children. Lord knows, Marsha wouldn't want to take any time out for a pregnancy.

We had been married for ten years. I think we thought we were in love when we decided to marry. Maybe I was the only one who thought he was in love. We'd met in a coffee shop at school. It was a cold rainy morning. I was alone at a table for two. Everywhere else was jammed. Marsha was looking for a place to sit, and I offered her the empty chair. We chatted a bit, introduced ourselves and made superficial conversation. That would have been it, but it started to rain heavily and the wind was blowing, so we ended up staying about an hour. One coffee morning turned into three, then, it was a date. We'd married, perhaps, because we were the ones each knew best, and college graduation was coming up.

As our marriage went on, it seemed that my wife's only interest in the marriage was to present the picture of the successful American business woman; husband, home - all the trappings. She might have also had a child or two, but it would have taken time out of her business life to actually get pregnant and deliver children. I doubted that if we had children that she would take time out of her business life to care for them. That would have been day care, a nanny, or me. During my more cynical times, I thought about getting life-sized, cardboard photographs of children, so our Christmas cards would look like the perfect family. She could do the same with me, but who would do the shopping, cleaning, and all the other chores?

A snowplow rumbled down the street, carving a single channel and connecting us, once again, to the outside world. Of course, the snowplow piled up a sizable amount of snow on the recently cleared sidewalk. So, I went out again and used the snow blower to clear the end of our, and Valerie's, drive and connect the clear area to the cleared area created by the snowplow.

Within an hour, Marsha was headed to the office. She was in a bad mood because the snow – beautiful as it was to the rest of the world – would make for a slow day in the real estate trade. I hated to admit it to myself, but I was almost glad to have her out of the house. Today, when she left, she was wearing black slacks and a traditional Norwegian sweater. Black clog ankle boots completed the look. I always took note.

At some time in the past, I discovered what she wore usually had something to do with her day's events. If she was going to show a house to a woman, her attire was completely professional. If it was a couple, she might wear something a bit more daring, but not unprofessional. The skirt a bit shorter or the slacks would be a bit tighter, and she had a couple of blouses that with the top button undone showed a hint of cleavage.

If she was going to show a house to a man alone, the slacks would be tailored to show off her derriere, and the second button on the above-mentioned blouse would be undone – allowing for a clear view of her breasts, especially if she bent over to point out something in a brochure. And, maybe a small pendant to draw the eye, like a fishing lure, if her prospect somehow missed her breasts at first and actually looked at the brochure.

She'd leave, I'd mark down what she was wearing, and at night I would ask her about her day. She was always eager to talk about her business and her business conquests. In the vast majority of cases, I was on the mark. She never asked about my work.

I don't believe she ever went beyond showing off a bit, although I wouldn't put it past her to "bump" into a male client accidentally if it would help close the deal. I could almost hear her, "Oh, I'm sorry. This space is a bit snug, but I know you'll love this place, and it isn't like there will always be two people passing here." I figured those times were pretty rare. She wouldn't do anything that might reflect poorly on the agency and herself – even if she wasn't above a little enticement.

I wasn't sure about today. The storm had thrown a curve into my prediction. And, maybe she had gotten a cancellation.

My mind wandered, and I had to wonder why small places were always "snug" or "cozy" if you were being enticed to buy. If the agent was trying to knock your price down, "snug" or "cozy" became "small," "tight," or even "claustrophobic." I shrugged it off, made myself some breakfast, showered quickly, then retired to my office on the second floor, to check e-mails and work on the projects I had.

One e-mail was from an account I didn't recognize. The subject line read, 'Thank you.' I opened the e-mail, and it read, 'Thank you, again, for your help this morning. If it weren't for you, I'd still be out there - freezing. Also, thank you for the advice on my project. It will help a lot.' It was signed, 'V.' I sent a simple, 'You're more than welcome.' Then, I got on with my workday.

Three

January turned into February, and as much as I don't generally like February, it was a beautiful month. Aside from the snow, which made the landscape look pristine, the air was clear and, for the most part, not too cold. Warmer air and the sun, following our storm, helped to clear much of the snow. Patches remained where the sun was blocked. Spring was on the way.

Sensing there might be an opportunity in our little neighborhood, Marsha decided to throw a party at our house – for selected neighbors who might be interested in listing with her. And if not them, maybe they knew somebody who knew somebody. The guest list included about twenty couples. The invitations said casual.

While Marsha was off doing her thing, I made sure that the house was spotless and the wine and food were ordered and delivered. The big day arrived – she had decided on a Friday night – and the weather had warmed. The evening was warm enough to be outside, and a fire in the firepit would make the outdoors more inviting. Of course, that served to spread the guests out and make catering to them a little more difficult. That was my job, as my wife spent her time schmoozing and impressing. She made sure all her "trophies" for her real estate prowess were displayed tastefully, but prominently, in the den, or family room. It made me wonder if you actually have to have a family to have a 'family room.'

Marsha wore professionally-tailored black slacks, a white silk blouse, and a gray long sweater that was open in the front – easily dumped if the house got too warm. *Professional*, I thought, *best not to get too tempting, after all, we were serving alcohol.*

Valerie's parents were invited. I don't think they had any inclination to sell, but my wife hoped they might know someone, or at the very least, I don't think she wanted to invite the rest of the neighbors and not them. Because there was a lot of territory to cover and hors d'oeuvres to restock on the trays, my wife provided me some assistance. She was paying Valerie ten dollars an hour to help out. Maybe she invited Valerie's parents because she didn't have a way to hire Valerie and not invite them. To Valerie's credit, she worked hard, kept everything (except the alcohol) stocked, and was almost invisible.

Halfway through the evening, I ran into Valerie's mom. "Good evening," I said.

"Oh, hello," she responded. "I don't know how your wife does it all."

"It all?" I asked.

"Yes, this house is spotless. And the food and wine are excellent. The guests are taken care of, AND she has time to go around to meet and talk with everyone. All this, and her business, too."

Tempted as I was to point out that all of the 'stuff' she had mentioned before "talking with everyone," had been taken care of by me, I didn't say anything.

"It was so nice of her to invite us. We aren't even thinking of selling."

"Well," I responded, "this isn't strictly for business. It is a meet and greet – a get to know you – party. We just want folks to meet each other and have a good time." *And, of course, if you happen to know of someone who is thinking of selling, you might just mention my wife.*

"That's so nice of her," she talked to me like I was the hired help.

"Where is your husband?" I asked.

"Fantasy football. It is like it takes up the entire year. It's a passion for him. He spends hours on it."

I thought that with football season behind us, fantasy football would be as well, at least for the time being, but I had no time for, or interest in football, fantasy or otherwise. So, I didn't know whether there was any 'off season' activity for fantasy football.

"Oh, by the way," she continued, "Valerie really appreciated you helping her with the snow. She was half frozen – not wearing the proper shoes and gloves, and all."

"It was my pleasure," I answered. "Besides, the snow blower made short work of it."

"Valerie also said you gave her some ideas for her school project. I'd hate to see her taken advantage of."

Alarm bells were going off somewhere in the back of my head. "How so?" I asked.

"Well, she has to work with two other girls, and I know they will try to dump all of the work onto her."

The alarm bells became quieter, but were not gone altogether. "I'm sure she will be able to manage that."

"Well, if you could help her a little bit with the who-does-what part, so she isn't overloaded, we would appreciate it."

"I'd be happy to," was my response.

"Because, you know, Valerie has things she has to do with the house. I, of course, get breakfast and get her off to school and Bill off to work." She said it like it was some giant chore, cooking, dressing them, and everything else. "And after school, we have her cook dinner – so she can learn how, you know – and I'm so tired of being out all day, and of course, Bill is tired after work, as well. Then, she has to clean the kitchen after dinner before doing her homework. So, if the other girls take advantage of her, she may not have time for the important things at home."

Again, I said, "Of course, I'd be happy to help her." I tried not to roll my eyes. I handed her one of my business cards and said, "Just have her send me an e-mail or text, and we can set up a time to meet." Apparently, there were at least two more people taking advantage of Valerie, and they didn't want 'her time' taken up by any others. I started to feel sorry for the girl who lived next door.

And, then Valerie's mom was off to tell my wife what a great party this was and what a wonderful job she had done.

Valerie – A Love Story

The rest of the evening was uneventful. Valerie offered to stay after the party and help clean up, but I told her I could do it myself. I gave her a hundred dollars, which made her eyes pop open, and I sent her home.

Anna Leigh

Four

I received and e-mail from Valerie asking if we could meet to talk about her project. I suggested the following Sunday morning, about 10 AM, and asked where she would like to meet. She asked if she could come to my house – she said she would explain. So, our meeting was on for 10 AM, Sunday.

Sunday morning, I got up, showered, shaved, and dressed in faded jeans and a gray sweatshirt. I wore my comfortable new fleece-lined house slippers for warmth. I fixed breakfast and cleaned the kitchen. My wife got up, showered, and dressed for church. Professional garb, no need to look like a hussy.

She wasn't a religious person, but she said attending church gave her that many more contacts for her real estate business. I almost never attended, which my wife explained away – "He has to work most Sundays." I would have told her that lying in church probably didn't pave the way to heaven, but she wouldn't have understood, and truth be told, it worked for her, and it worked for me.

It was still winter, and colder air had returned. Most of the snow from the previous storm had melted, although there were still patches in the shady spots the sun didn't warm during the day. Brown grass covered the parts of the lawn that were visible. High thin clouds filtered the sunlight and made the day a bright-ish gray.

I had just made my second cup of coffee when there was a quiet tapping on the patio door. Valerie was wearing a fluffy pink sweater and jeans. She had block-heeled short boots on her feet that she took off and left at the door when she entered. She looked cold.

"Something to drink?" I asked.

"Do you have something warm?"

"Coffee, tea, or hot chocolate?"

Valerie opted for the hot chocolate. I warned her that it was instant. She said that was fine, then changed it to "perfect."

While I made the chocolate, we talked about her project.

"The class was split into groups of three," she started. "Each group is supposed to report on a place in Medieval Europe. The reports are supposed to be between 15 and 20 pages." She said the last part with a little concern in her voice. "Anyway, I'm hoping you can help me figure out how to make a plan so that it gets done, and, almost as important, so that three people in my group don't get the credit for work that only I have done."

"That should be do-able," I said. I finished making her hot chocolate and added a few small marshmallows. We sat at the counter in the kitchen. I opened my laptop and started a new document. "First things first. When do you have to have this finished – to turn in?" I put down the date. Then, I decided that for visual reference, we could draw out an actual time line on paper, and pulled out a legal pad. We put the finish date at the right side and the start date, today, on the left.

I started to talk about planning sessions, reporting, research, and the details of the plan before we actually wrote anything down.

We didn't get very far before I noticed Valerie was wrapping herself around the hot chocolate in an effort to keep warm. While house wasn't toasty, I didn't think it was cold.

"Why don't we move into the den," I suggested.

"You can barely get into our den," she replied, somewhat quietly.

"Why?"

"My dad has all his sports stuff all over the place. There is barely anyplace to sit. That's why I asked if we could meet here. Your place is really neat and clean. And, of course, my dad is always watching sports or reading about sports in the paper. The other reason is my mom. She always seems to be distracted by her upcoming social thing. And until she is ready to go out the door, she looks pretty much like she was standing next to a car that blew up."

I laughed in spite of myself. "It can't be that bad."

"Well, you are so nice to help me with this, and I couldn't ask you to go through that." As she said it, she looked over toward her house. Then, she smiled. "Well, it isn't an actual war zone, but this is much better."

I punched the button on the gas fireplace, and the flame sprang to life.

"That is SO cool," she said. She seemed honestly surprised.

"Here, take these." I doffed my slippers figuring I would be warm enough with feet covered in thick socks. After a short protest, she accepted, and sat on a padded stool near the fire. After a bit, she started to relax, the fire, chocolate, and slippers warming her.

"So, tell me about the group you are working with."

"Three girls, thank god," she said. "I'm so glad it isn't two boys, or even one. They aren't serious, they don't want to work, and all they do is make stupid comments – about sex and stuff – and gawk. Or, they're jocks and think all the girls should just 'roll over' for them. The other girls in my group are okay, but I don't want to be stuck with all the work."

Over the next hour, we put together a plan and a timeline, with the work shared. Valerie, who had gotten all As in English would do the writing. That would be the main work at the end, so the other girls would be doing most of the research. Valerie decided to highlight everyday life in Medieval times. She thought about a small village and all the things that went on there, as well as their problems. We even put together a plan for the research and the time to complete it. In the end, I coached her through some limits, because this could easily go much longer than twenty pages.

"You should try to meet at least once a week," I said, "and send a report of your weekly progress to your teacher. That way, you can keep track of your progress, AND it will be an incentive to the other girls not to fall behind."

"That's a great idea," said Valerie.

Valerie had a second cup of chocolate, even though she said, "This isn't going to do my 'figure' any good." I told her not to worry. As she sipped it, she talked about herself.

"I got mono a few years ago. It really hit me hard, and I ended up having to repeat a grade because I missed so much of the year. So, now I'm older than most of my class. I'll be twenty this year. Some of the kids call me grand ma. It kind of hurts. Of course, my dad only said, 'Well, life throws curve balls from time to time.' He'll probably have some sports thing written on his tomb stone. Maybe something about the final curve ball taking him out."

I told her that if she were 'grand ma', they must think I'm Methuselah. Of course, then I had to explain who Methuselah was.

Valerie sipped her second cup of hot chocolate slowly. She found Jim, Mr. Connor, interesting. He talked to her like she was an equal and he was interested in what she had to say. He seemed to actually care about her, what she said, and what she thought. She looked at him more closely. Without all his outside clothing on, the thick trousers and jacket, he appeared trim. She found herself wondering what he looked like – not without clothing, but whether he was soft or muscular.

We had a lovely conversation, but Valerie said she had things she needed to do. I put the plan into an e-mail that I sent to Valerie. I also gave her all the paper we created. After she left, I sat in front of the fire, relaxed, and thought about the girl next door. I knew almost nothing about Valerie before that morning, but I realized that there were many assumptions I had made about the teenager and most of those weren't correct. She was a lovely young woman, intelligent and working pretty hard, in school and at home. Her carefree and easy life wasn't quite as fun or easy as it might appear from the outside.

After a while, my mind drifted to when I was 16, sitting in my room, trying to finish my homework. If Valerie's dad was virtually 'absent' while he was there – lost in his sports world – my dad was physically absent. He sold insurance, and when he wasn't doing that, he was at the country club, playing golf, making new contacts, and drinking. He once joked that he belonged to a drinking club with a golf problem. My mom tried her best, but was buried in a loveless marriage and developed her own coping mechanisms. They included arguments with dad about the amount of time he spent away. I vowed to leave as soon as I graduated and turned 18. That's how I found myself in the recruiter's office, then on a plane, then in boot camp in San Diego. I joined the Navy and was going to see the world. While boot camp wasn't a lot of fun, I had a sense of belonging for the first time I could remember.

Dear Diary,

Today I went to our neighbor's house – Jim Connor – so he could help me with my history project. He was really, really nice. I was cold, so he made me hot chocolate - twice (It will probably make me fat.) and started a fire so I could warm up. He even gave me his slippers. He treated me like he and I were equals, not like I was a child. He showed me how to do the work so it would be shared. I had a really great time. He was so nice. Oh, and he looks like he might be in good shape. And, he's kinda cute.

Five

Valerie contacted me via e-mail a couple of times over the next few weeks. She had a few questions, but she was working the plan perfectly, and things were coming together. She ended up doing some of the research, just to make sure the paper and presentation were completed on time. She started writing drafts earlier than she thought she would be able to. In the end, she told me that the twenty pages turned out to be much easier than she thought it ever would be.

Eight weeks after our planning meeting, she knocked on the patio door. I left my office, went into the kitchen and to the door. She looked like a kid on Christmas morning.

"We got an A+!!" she fairly shouted. "An A+! Nobody else in the class came close! And YOU did it! It was so much easier with your help. Thank you! Thank you!"

"Wait a minute," I interrupted. "I helped you structure your project. Your A+ was because of what YOU did, not me. And, by the way, congratulations. You did a great job."

"I couldn't have done it without your help," she said, and gave me a big hug.

I protested, saying that it was her work, and again, I said I just helped with some structure. Then, I asked if I could read the report.

"You want to read it?" she asked. "I didn't think you would want to read it. I'm not sure it is that good."

"Are you kidding," I answered, "it is an A+ report. You don't get a chance to read many of those."

She ran home and returned with the report. She said she had to run, but wanted to know what I thought. "Don't be too hard on my report," she said.

When she was gone, I sat in the den and read the report. Instead of writing a boring tome on life in the Medieval ages, she had written a story about two early teens and their family. The family lived on a small farm on the outskirts of a large village. After writing about life on the small farm, the girls, Sophie and Sadie, venture into the village to buy things for an upcoming celebration. On the way, they describe life in the village, the tradecraft, the trials and tribulations of living in that time. She had done an excellent job. The story was clear, engaging, and tightly written. It was worth at least an A+.

I saw her the next day and told her, "This is really great! They should make something higher than A+ just for this."

She giggled and said, "You aren't just saying that so you won't hurt my feelings, are you?"

Then, it was my turn. "I think you just want me to tell you again how great it really is. I've paid for many books that weren't nearly this good."

She hugged me and said, "Thank you. Thank you. Thank you." Then, she was gone.

Six

Spring was in full swing and summer was approaching. My wife decided that her first party worked so well that it was time for another at our place. This one was to drum up more contacts or cement the relationships with promising contacts from the previous soiree. I did the cleaning, etc. My wife wanted this to look like a grand event and was kind enough to hire Valerie, again, at $10 an hour, to help out, serve the guests, and make sure the dirty plates and napkins, etc., were picked up. Valerie and I both wore black slacks, pale blue shirts, and matching red bow ties. I had to tie Valerie's.

Valerie's parents didn't attend this time. I don't really know whether they weren't invited or they just chose not to attend – maybe they had no intention of selling their home, and they felt attending would be taking something for nothing. Valerie didn't seem to mind that her parents weren't attending, in fact, she seemed brighter if anything. The group attending was relatively large, but not unmanageable. Valerie, as before, was working as if she were dedicated to the job.

The weather was cool, but not too cool, and we lit the firepit. We had asked anyone who smoked to do that on the patio. The firepit was lit to help keep those smoking warm, and it seemed to be a draw for everyone, because a number of guests, smokers and non-smokers alike, were chatting outside.

The guests on the patio needed more wine, and I was coming out of the kitchen with a bottle of red and one of white. I was looking in one direction and traveling in another when I bumped into someone. It turned out to be Valerie, headed in the opposite direction. We bumped front to back – my front and her, um, back.

As I opened my mouth to say something, Valerie blushed, smiled and said, "Oops! I'm sorry. I should have been watching where I was going."

I should have been watching where I was going, as well, but I couldn't exactly say I was sorry. A bit guilty, perhaps, but not sorry. A part of me actually started to react. *For Christ sake*, I thought, *she's too young. Control yourself.*

The party was dull and belonged to someone else. Working with Valerie was actually the best part.

This party dragged on. Guests seemed to stay longer. Maybe not. Maybe it just seemed that way when I was working with a group of people I didn't really know for a business I didn't really care about. Well, it was a business that was coming between my wife and me.

The house finally started to clear out, and I was able to start getting the kitchen together. Valerie insisted in staying to help. Marsha was camped out in the living room with a small group that wanted to sit and chat.

Valerie and I were in the kitchen. I was clearing plates and putting them into the sink, in order to clean them before they went into the dishwasher. The wine glasses had been washed and sat on the mat, draining.

"I'm trying to decide what to do after I graduate from high school," Valerie began. She was drying the wine glasses and putting them into the cupboard. "What did you do?"

"Uh, I joined the Navy."

"Can I ask why?"

"Yes."

I think she rolled her eyes. "Why?"

I was trying not to say that it was the quickest way to get out of the house and away. "We didn't really have money for college, and the Navy was a job and a way to get an education."

"Your parents didn't have money to send you to college?"

Again, I tried to give an answer that wasn't a lie, but wasn't entirely truthful either. I didn't want to say that my parents had money for country clubs, golf, shopping, and a lot of other things, but they didn't value their son's continuing education enough to put even a little money aside. "Uh, no. There were issues." I hoped that would suffice.

"So, what did you do in the Navy?" she asked.

"I was a corpsman."

"A what?"

"Corpsman – the Army and Air Force call them medics. In the Navy, they are corpsmen. Mostly, you assist doctors and nurses, and perform other medical tasks, but on some ships and some very small bases, the corpsman is the only medical care."

"Were you ever the only medical care?

"No. I was on a ship with a doctor and two other corpsmen."

"What was it like – on a ship."

"I thought it was a good time. You become close to the other sailors. It's funny, but when you come into port, you end up going out with the guys you just spent months with at sea. There were both good times and difficult times on the ship; mostly good times, but things happened that were definitely not good."

"What were the good things?"

"Like I mentioned, you work and live with a group of guys that you grow very close to. It is a brotherhood. I haven't found anything like it in the civilian world. And, you get to work with some great technology. It's funny, I didn't really have anyone to go back to, and I enjoyed being on the ship at sea."

"So, what were the bad – or not-good – things."

"Sometimes you have to see and do things that nobody should ever have to see or do." A memory was returning, resurfacing. A memory I wanted to forget, but never would.

"Like what?"

Anna Leigh

"I'm not sure I should be talking about this with you," although in some strange way, I felt like she was someone I could talk to. She was open and accepting. I wanted to tell her and I didn't. Years ago, when I started to tell Marsha about this memory, she listened superficially and dismissed the experience with, "Well, things like that happen all the time in the military, I suppose." It had been a terrible experience, it had affected me deeply, and I hadn't brought it up again. But I didn't really want to burden this young lady with my experience – and what I considered my failing.

"Why not? Have you told anyone else?"

"That person didn't want to listen." I was trying to bury the memory, but it wasn't working.

Valerie had stopped what she was doing. She was leaning with her back against the counter, looking at me. "I want to listen," she said. "It sounds like you need someone to listen – really listen. And, if you don't, I'll be like a splinter in your finger. I'll be a real pain until you tell me." She had a look in her eyes of someone who truly wanted to listen. She told me later that the look in my eyes was of sadness and pain.

I remember the day as if it were yesterday. I was on a ship, three days out of home port – San Diego – and heading home after a deployment. The sun was shining and there was a breeze; enough to kick up four to five-foot waves. The water was the deepest blue you can imagine. I had just returned from lunch and plopped down in a chair in sick bay. Then, an alarm sounded and a few seconds later the whole ship shuddered. There was a low 'whump' that reverberated throughout the ship.

"There was an explosion in the engine room," I said. "One of the fuel lines sprung a pinhole leak. That causes the fuel under pressure to atomize as it squirts from the line. So, there is a fine mist of fuel in the air. Dangerous, very dangerous."

"Was anybody hurt?" Valerie asked.

"There were four people in the engine room at the time. When the senior man – a chief – saw the leak, he hit the alarm then ordered all doors and hatches closed."

"Why?" she asked quietly.

"Because he knew that if the fuel exploded, and the exits weren't closed, the fire would spread to the rest of the ship. He – they – gave their lives to save the ship."

I couldn't say anymore for at least a minute. Maybe it was longer. When I looked up, Valerie had tears in her eyes and a tear running down her cheek.

"And you knew those men."

"Yes. Some I liked; some I didn't like as much. But they were all shipmates. And they gave their lives so the rest of us could live. I'm not sure I deserved that."

By now, Valerie was crying. I said I should stop, but she hugged me, put her face on my chest, and told me I'd better not stop. I moved her to one of the kitchen chairs.

"The fire party was already opening the engine room door when I arrived. They were spraying water on the door, then into the compartment. It took a while to knock down the fire. The engine room has a system that is supposed to put the fire out completely, but the fire wasn't all the way out. The different levels in the engine room –

the floors - are made out of grates. You can see all the way to the bottom of the space – through those grates. There was a lot of smoke in the air. It was hard to see."

I remembered entering the engine room, looking down and seeing water sloshing around below the grating. Various bits of debris and trash were floating in the water. The sailors who work the engine room keep it spotless. I remember thinking that their work had been destroyed. The air was thick with smoke, and various areas of the walls, machinery, and ceiling were charred. The engine room was usually warm, that day it was almost unbearably hot. When the fuel exploded, it must have been true hell.

"It must have been scary."

"Yes, I was scared."

"Were – were the men who – had . . ." she was searching for the right words.

I was wearing a mask, an oxygen breathing apparatus, usually called an OBA, so I didn't smell anything different while I had it on. There were charred forms that were once human beings, human beings who I had known and worked with. The forms were unrecognizable. In one corner, a form was partially hidden. I walked over and saw a body. Half his face was burned beyond recognition. On the side of his face, his features were still recognizable. It was a shocking reminder that this had been a friend, a shipmate, now dead. My mind didn't want to accept the reality, but I couldn't deny this. I started to vomit, but to do so, I had to pull off my mask. I vomited, and again. Each time I vomited I sucked smoke-filled air into my lungs that was contaminated, had little oxygen, and smelled of burnt human flesh. I vomited a third time, inhaled, and the world went black.

"They were all dead," I said. "Killed when the fuel exploded." And burned, mostly beyond recognition.

"Oh my God!" Valerie said. "That's terrible! That must have been awful. What did you do?"

"I took off my oxygen mask to vomit. The contaminated air, the smoke, and the lack of oxygen made me pass out." I left out the part about the smell of burnt human flesh. "I woke up in sick bay six hours later."

Valerie was staring at me. She said, "I can't imagine how terrible it must be to have had to do what you did."

"Going into a disaster scene and doing your duty is part of the job. Throwing up and passing out isn't."

"I – you," clearly, she was searching for words again.

"As far as I'm concerned, that isn't the worst part," I continued.

"WHAT could be worse than that?" she asked.

"When it was all over, my shipmates treated me like, well, not quite like a hero, but nobody faulted me or gave me a hard time about puking or passing out. The Navy gave the engine room crew who died posthumous medals for bravery and for saving the ship. They deserved them. They gave the fire crew, including me, medals for putting out the fire, etc. I didn't deserve one and tried to refuse mine, but they gave it to me anyway, and I was ordered to wear it. I considered it my 'badge of shame.' Every time I see it, I think of brave men and know my having it is a fraud."

I sat in a chair for a moment. Valerie got up, walked over, kissed me on the top of my head, pulled my head against her chest, and said, "I can't believe you went through all that. I can't believe nobody has listened."

"Truth be told," I said getting up, "I don't tell all that many people that story. It's not a part of my life I want to remember."

"I'm glad you told me," she said. "I'm glad you trusted me."

I gave Valerie a hundred dollars for her night's work. She tried to refuse, but I told her that therapists charge a lot more. I tried to smile. I'm not sure I pulled it off. She relented, kissed me on the cheek, and left for home. As I watched her go, I no longer saw her as the little girl next door. She was a woman I had trusted with a part of me that I didn't often show to anyone, and she had responded with warmth, understanding, and compassion. I wondered if that was too much to expect.

I turned off the lights – the rest of the guests had finally departed – and headed upstairs. As my wife undressed, she regaled me with her successes that night and told me how she had at least ten new prospects. I went to my second-floor office to check on a couple of things, and I have to admit, to get away from Marsha for a few minutes. When I went in, there was a piece of paper on my laptop. I opened it as saw a handwritten note.

It merely said, "I wasn't really sorry for bumping into you. I'm glad it happened. V"

I sat in the dark of my office. The memory wasn't completely gone. I had rotated off the ship shortly after the fire – my normal rotation – but I couldn't get rid of the memory or the sense of failure. Once on shore, I got a small place off-base, and picked up my personal possessions from storage. Among them was a 45-caliber automatic pistol. I loaded it, got a bottle of scotch, and sat looking at it for a long, long time. I felt like a complete failure.

Before I could decide what I was going to do, there was a knock on my door. I hid the pistol in a drawer. A chief petty officer, a senior enlisted man I knew from the ship, was on the other side of the door when I opened it up. He said he had come over to check on me. He told me that he'd seen a look I had in my eyes that he had seen in other men's eyes before, and it didn't mean good things.

We talked, and after that night, I had gotten into therapy – with a psychologist who I credit with being a miracle worker. He got me through it, but there were times when the old sense of failure and the desire to end it all came back.

Anna Leigh

Dear Diary,

Tonight, I worked a party at the Connor's. The work wasn't very hard, really, and I literally bumped into Mr. Connor (Jim) coming out of the kitchen. I said I was sorry, but I wasn't really. I actually had to time it right so we would collide. I thought it would be fun. As it turned out, once we collided, it became more than just fun – for me, anyway. I don't know about him, but he did have a surprised look on his face. I left a note in his office. I hope he isn't mad about that.

Later, when we were cleaning up, he told me about something terrible that happened when he was in the Navy. It was so sad – and he was so upset about what he thinks he did wrong – it made me cry. But I'm glad he trusted me and told me. He has done a lot for me and I want to help him, too. It sure doesn't seem like he gets much help from his wife.

P.S – He WAY overpaid me again.

Seven

Valerie came over the next day. She tried to give the hundred dollars back, saying she didn't deserve 'all that.' I told her she did and I wouldn't take it back.

She finally changed the subject. "I'm having a graduation celebration on Saturday. It's actually before graduation, if that makes any sense, but I'd have to really screw up to not graduate now. If I gave a party, would you come?"

"First," I started, "I'm not sure I'd fit in with your friends."

"Well," she said, "there really aren't going to be any friends there. I know a few girls, but we'll get together for something after school next week. My 'party'," she drew out the word party, "will pretty much be my parents, and you know what a wild time that will be."

"I'd love to," I continued, "but I don't think your parents would really approve of me coming to your private party. Besides, I look terrible in one of those little party hats.

She laughed harder than I thought she would. When she stopped, she said, "Can you imagine my parents

Anna Leigh

and you sitting around a table with me and everybody wearing those stupid pointy hats? I can't get the image out of my mind. I'm going to send you an invitation anyway – just to show you I'd really like you to be there. Even if you can't."

The invitation arrived the next day. Hand-made, it was beautiful. I could tell it took some work to get it done. I had her e-mail address, so I apologized for sending my 'regrets' via e-mail and told her that as much as I would like to attend, it probably would be better if I didn't. She replied that she would be disappointed, but that she would save me a piece of cake – if there even was one.

The day before her party, I asked her to come over so I could give her something. I gave her a card that contained a hundred dollars, and I told her that she couldn't open it until the next day.

The afternoon of her party, Valerie was at the patio door. She had my card in her hand. She gave me a hug and a kiss on the cheek. She said about ten 'Thank you-s,' kissed me quickly on the lips and said she had to get back to her 'party,' such as it was. The kiss surprised me. In retrospect, it made me feel something I hadn't felt in a long time – a feeling of romance. That made me feel a little guilty. I know I didn't initiate the kiss, but I felt guilty because I enjoyed it.

On Sunday morning, I was in the kitchen, sipping a cup of tea. Valerie stopped by. She had an envelope and a little box.

"Good morning, celebration girl," I said.

"That was yesterday, but thank you. And thank you, again, for the gift."

"I only wish it had been more," I replied.

First, she looked surprised, then her face took on an impish look. "Really?" She drew the word out for five seconds. "How much more?" She paused before she said, "Never mind. It was perfect. My parents gave me a fifty-dollar gift certificate to a clothing store. I guess they don't like the way I dress."

"You might want to use it to get some decent gloves and boots for the next snow," I kidded.

She didn't bat an eye. "Don't need to. There is a great guy next door. He has a snow blower and will come to my rescue."

"Touché," I said.

"So, anyway," again she drew out the word anyway. "A piece of cake is in the box. You can eat that now, if you want. The card is a thank you for your gift."

"You already thanked me about a hundred times."

"Yes, but this is the official thank you," she drew out the word official. She put her hand on my upper arm as she talked. *It feels so nice just to touch him*, she thought.

Valerie paused, and I heard myself saying, "I'm not sure I can eat all of the cake you brought me. Why don't you sit down with me and we can share this?"

"So," she said, "you actually want me fat."

"With your metabolism and activity, you'll burn this off in no time. I'M the one who has to worry about getting fat."

"Uh huh. Is that what you tell all the girls?"

"You're all the girls." I startled myself as I said that. It hinted that maybe we were a thing. I didn't want it to sound that way.

"Well, in that case, I might just share a bite or two."

I opened the box. It was a fair-sized piece of her celebration cake. Chocolate with white frosting. It was a corner piece, and there was a squiggle around the edge. I lifted the cake out with a spatula and set it on a plate. I was about to cut it into two pieces when Valerie stopped me.

"You might give me more than I can eat," she said. "We can just share the one piece."

Somehow, sharing this piece of cake began to feel intimate.

I retrieved two forks from the drawer, and we sat next to each other, and facing, next to the counter. The cake was actually very good.

Valerie took a bite. "So, no other girls?" she asked.

"No. No other girls."

"I was just wondering about my competition."

"You don't have any – wait – what? What I mean is . . . '

Valerie just giggled. "Tongue tied? You sound a bit flustered."

I laughed. Maybe I was.

Valerie cut off a smallish sized piece of the cake. She looked at it for a second or two, then caught my gaze. Her fork moved to my mouth. Her eyes were locked on mine. They seemed to twinkle. A very small smile was on her lips. I opened my mouth, and she carefully, and slowly, placed the cake.

"There, wasn't that nice?" she asked.

All I could do was look at her. Flustered and tongue-tied I was.

"Can't decide?" she continued. "You must need more." She lifted a second small piece from the plate. If anything, she moved her fork to my mouth more slowly than before, and it took longer than before to place it just where she wanted it.

Without waiting, she picked up a third piece, and said, "Third time's the charm."

Her look, her touch, her eyes, her voice – I was getting aroused by this young lady feeding me cake.

"Well, it looks like you are enjoying it. Why don't you try?"

I picked up my fork, cut a small piece from the corner, and tried not to show how much I was shaking. Valerie's eyes never left mine. Her mouth opened slowly. When I put the cake into her mouth, she closed her lips around the fork and held it there for a few seconds. Not only was I aroused, I was starting to breathe a little faster.

"Would you," I had to clear my throat, "would you like something to drink?" I managed to ask.

Valerie picked up the cup with my tea in it and said, "If you're not afraid of cooties, I'll just take a sip of this. Okay?"

Anna Leigh

I nodded. She sipped – all the time with her eyes on mine. It seemed like she was looking into my soul. I was totally exposed to her and vulnerable, but I didn't care. I knew she wouldn't hurt me. I felt a tingle run through me – a realization that I could trust someone that much.

She fed me another bite and with her eyes asked me to feed her. "Well," she said with an enchanting look, "I guess conversation is out, at least until we finish the cake." She sipped a bit more of my tea.

It took more than ten minutes to finish the cake. We traded feeding each other small bites. The only time Valerie's eyes left mine were when she would look to pick up a bite of cake for me. When she did, she would close her lids slowly when she looked down, and close and open them slowly as she lifted her gaze and caught my eyes once she had the bit of cake on her fork.

There were only a few bites left. Valerie slid a small piece into my mouth, a piece of frosting caught on my lip. I was about to lick it off when Valerie stopped me. "Huh uh." She reached over and removed it with her finger. Then, she licked it off the end of her finger.

"I missed some," she said, and presented a perfectly manicured finger to me. From which I licked the remainder of the frosting. I was totally mesmerized.

It took a few more minutes to finish the cake. I think we may have been cutting smaller and smaller bites. Finally, it was gone.

"I hope you're happy," she said. "I'll probably get fat, then, you'll just find somebody else."

I just sat staring.

"You're quiet. Are you thinking about me getting fat?" Then, "I hope I didn't upset you, sharing the cake, well, like that."

It took me a minute to say, "Upset? No, I'm not upset. I'm, well, uh . . ."

Valerie giggled.

"Stunned," is all I could get out.

"I don't really go out very much, but I've never actually 'stunned' anyone before," she said. "Actually, I never even tried. But you're different. Something about you makes me feel safe. And warm. You really care."

"Well, okay," she continued taking a final sip of my tea. "I need to do a couple of things, but I hate to leave. I really enjoyed sharing your, or my," she giggled, again, "our cake."

Valerie got up. I started to. She looked at me and said, "Oh, missed a spot." With that, she put her lips on mine. I felt the tip of her soft tongue lick off an imaginary bit of frosting.

I walked Valerie to the patio door.

"Thank you for the cake, Valerie. I don't think I've ever enjoyed a piece of cake as much as I enjoyed sharing that one." *Smooth*.

"I liked it at least as much as you did. But you did seem awfully quiet."

"Stunned," was all I could say.

Valerie smiled, maybe there was a small laugh. She put her hand on my chest – it seemed like I felt it in my heart. "I've got to go work this off," she said, "I'll see you, gosh, I don't know, but I hope it isn't too long." Then, she was gone.

I watched her until she was out of view. I felt excited – and guilty. Of course, if asked, I could say that the girl – girl, she is a woman – next door brought over a piece of cake from her graduation party. And, we chatted while we split and ate it. In reality, I knew that was a lie. We had shared something very intimate. It left me aroused, excited, and wanting to see her again. More than just stunned, I was smitten. And, in trouble.

Marsha returned from her networking trip to church about two hours later. She went on about who she had met and the possibilities of sales. After about twenty minutes, she off-handedly asked if anything had happened that morning.

"Um, the neighbor girl, Valerie, came over to thank us for the graduation gift we gave her."

"We gave her a – a what? A graduation gift?"

"Yes. She mentioned she was graduating when we were helping out with your party."

"Oh. Well, that was nice. Maybe the parents will remember when . . . I hope our gift wasn't too large." She said it like it was actually *our* gift.

"I didn't give her any more than what we paid her for working the party." Marsha didn't know I'd actually give Valerie a hundred dollars.

"That's okay, then. And she said 'Thank you?'"

"Um, yes."

Then, Marsha was back to talking about her newest church contacts. I hate to admit that over time, when she started to drone on about her business, I tended to tune her out.

Anna Leigh

Dear Diary,

Yesterday was my graduation party, well, more of a pre-graduation party. I don't actually graduate for a couple more weeks. The official party wasn't much. Mom and Dad, and a cake. They gave me a gift certificate for $50 – to get some clothes. Jim gave me $100. This morning, I took him a thank you note, and a piece of my party cake. Somehow, we decided to share it. I teased him about it making me fat, so we ate it off the same plate. Then, I decided to feed him, and I got him to feed me. It started as something funny, but it didn't take long before it was more. I think we were both kind of turned on – I know for sure I was, and I think he was, because his eyes changed – softer, loving, I don't know, I could just tell. Then, of course, he kind of lost the ability to talk. He was so cute. So, before I left, I kissed him – pretending there was some frosting left on his lips. I had a really great time. I can't wait to see him again.

Eight

A few days later, my phone rang. It was Valerie.

"I really hate to ask," she started, "you've done so much already, but I need a favor."

"You have to ask for the favor first. I can't agree without knowing what it is – in case you, say, want my brain for a school research project."

"Give me a chance, Silly," she continued, "although I'll have to think about the brain thing. I can always use extra credit. I have to have a wisdom tooth out, and the dentist says I need someone to drive me home. He says I'll be kind of dopey – even more than usual. My parents will be doing other things, so they can't get me."

"Um, sure. I'll be glad to drive you home. Do you need a ride there, too?"

"Well, I was going to take the bus."

"Now it's your turn to be silly, Valerie. I'll be happy to take you and bring you home."

"Thank you," she said. "I could really ride the bus."

Anna Leigh

"No," I said, "I will take you, as well."

"Thank you," she said quietly. "Ten o'clock, Friday morning, please. And, thank you, again."

Friday arrived. I got up, shaved and showered. Marsha left the house about nine. She was wearing Navy slacks that showed off her derriere in the best possible way, a relatively low-cut gray blouse, a small pendant, and four-inch heels. *Must be showing homes to a guy*, I thought.

I ate breakfast, had some coffee, and brushed my teeth. I wore faded jeans and a dark blue cotton sweater. Valerie came over about nine forty-five. She was wearing dark blue sweats that fit well but not too tight, and tennies. We were at the dentist's office before ten.

Valerie seemed nervous as she filled out her paperwork. She kept fidgeting her feet. I put my hand on hers and said, "I know you are scared, but it will be alright."

She said, "So, you'll protect me?"

"Yes, I'll protect you." I didn't know how I could do that, but I said it hoping it would make her feel better.

She had little time to sit, though; they were ready for her almost as soon as the papers were turned in.

"Wish me luck," she said as they walked her back to the operating suite.

The procedure took a little less than an hour. I spent my time looking through what I can only describe as archival copies of Newsweek magazine. An overweight nurse in green scrubs came into the waiting room and asked me to follow her. Her dark brown hair was covered in a green surgical bonnet. I was ushered into a dental office that looked more like an operating room, which I guess it was. There were IVs, monitoring machines, oxygen, and a lot of other things more at home in a surgical operating room than a dental office. There were no dental instruments in sight. The lighting was subdued.

Valerie was in the chair, reclining, and seemingly asleep. The nurse measured her blood pressure, pulse, and counted her respirations. The doctor came in shortly after. He took a quick look at the latest vital signs, then turned to me.

"Valerie said you would be the friend picking her up." I couldn't tell if it was a question or statement.

"Yes, her parents weren't available."

He seemed to think about that for a half a minute, then said, "Yes, that's what I understand. So, I've written out the post-operative instructions. As soon as you get her home, she should take one of these," he handed me a small bottle with eight pills in it. "They are for pain, and it is best to get ahead of it – start the medication before the pain starts. I'm not sure she will have much pain, but I want her to have one every six hours for the first day."

"Got it," I replied. "I'll get the first one into her."

"You might want to get something into her stomach. These make some people sick to their stomach."

"How about a milk shake or ice cream?" I asked.

"That would be okay, but you'll have to spoon the milkshake into her. I don't want her sucking on a straw – it could cause a dry socket, and that would be very painful."

I got Valerie to the car. She was walking, more or less, and semi-coherent. I went through a fast food drive through and got a chocolate milk shake. I had to wonder what the fast food staff thought of the guy with the half-conscious young woman next to him in the front seat. I hoped the ice pack on her jaw would convince them not to call the police.

When we got to her place, I parked, then helped her into the house. I found a spoon and started feeding her. She said she could do it herself, but she seemed to be having a bit of trouble with her coordination. Her mouth was eluding the end of the spoon. I got about half the milkshake into her, gave her the medication, then decided to put her to bed.

"I've got to get you upstairs and into bed."

"Okay. Upstairs."

We got to the top of the stairs, and I asked where her room was. She pointed.

Her room was definitely a girl's room. One wall was pink. The furniture was white. I think I saw a 'My Little Pony' on the dresser.

I helped her to her bed and had her sit. I untied her shoes and took them off. "That's about all I can do," I said. "You'll have to sleep in those," I motioned to her sweats. "I can't get you undressed and into your jammies."

She giggled and said the word 'jammies.' "That's okay," she said, "I'll be comfy in these. I don't have anything on underneath. Wanna see?"

"Um, no," I said quickly. "I don't think that would be appropriate."

"Appropriate?" she asked.

"Smart," I said.

"Because I'm only nineteen and we're alone in my bedroom and the dentist doped me up – oh yes, and you're married?" She was talking softly and sounding like she was a little loopy, but her thought processes seemed pretty much right on.

"I'd say that pretty much covers the bases."

"You don't have to worry about my dad shooting you," she said. "He doesn't even have a gun. Well, he might, but I don't think he has a gun. Do you have a gun?"

"Is that important?"

"I just wanted to know. You know. Oh well, even if I did get undressed, you'd probably think I wasn't worth looking at. Some of my parts are too big, some are too small – the ones that are big should be smaller and the ones that are small should be bigger – oh yes, some just don't, well, you know."

I didn't – not for sure, anyway. "Valerie, you are a beautiful young woman. You are perfect, just the way you are. Every woman since the beginning of time has thought some parts were too big, too small, or whatever. Mostly, they have been wrong. And the parts that are different a lot of times are what make the women all the more beautiful to the ones who love them."

"You aren't just saying that," she started.

"So, I won't hurt your feelings?" I finished. "No. I'm saying it because it is true. You are like the combination of an angel and," I was lost, "and another angel." I was beginning to wonder if the medication the doctor had given Valerie was affecting me as well.

"Two angels? Which two angels?"

"The two most beautiful angels. Now, you have to rest."

"Okay, but first, I have to tell you a secret. But I have to whisper it to you."

I went over to her and started to put my ear down to hear her whisper. Valerie wrapped her arms tightly around my neck and kissed me seductively for a good ten seconds. I was shocked and started to pull away, but she was wrapped tightly around my neck. Finally, I just relaxed. When she finally let me go, she said, "Actually, it was two secrets. The first one is, I've wanted to do that for a long time."

It took me a minute, but I asked, "And the second secret?" I was almost afraid of what the second secret might be, and I thought of running away, but that didn't seem very brave.

"Simple. I love you. You don't have to say anything back. You're married, and I'm just a little girl – although you did call me a woman a few times today – thank you for that – but I understand if you can't," she paused, "or don't want to say anything."

I gave her a soft kiss on her lips, then said, "I love you too, Valerie." As the words came out of my mouth, I realized two things. First, while I shouldn't have said it, I meant what I had said. Second, while this could be big trouble, I didn't feel regret.

"Now, get some rest." I think she said, 'Yes dear.' I shook my head in disbelief, left her room, went downstairs and placed the post-op instructions and medication where it should be easily found – by her mom. I didn't think her dad would pay any attention unless I put it into the racing form. I put my car into the garage, went into the house, and poured myself three fingers of scotch.

Anna Leigh

Dear Diary,

Yesterday, I had to have my wisdom tooth taken out. I was really scared. I asked Jim if he could pick me up, and he volunteered to take me too. I was really glad, because having him there made it better. The dentist gave me some medicine that made me sleepy. Jim drove me home and got a milkshake. I think it was so the medicine wouldn't make me sick. Anyway, I was still dopey when we got home, and I had Jim take me to my bedroom. The medicine made me not care as much as I usually do, so I grabbed Jim, then I really kissed him. I told him I love him, too. He said he loved be back. I don't know if it is really true, but I loved hearing him say it. I know he's married and we shouldn't be — or I shouldn't be wanting him, but I really do love him. I hope he does love me and that he doesn't get into trouble.

Nine

It was a few weeks later, and the weather was warm. I was out finishing some work on the yard, getting ready for the summer. I looked over the fence and saw Valerie on her patio. She is in her late teen years, pretty (which girls don't like to be called). Her breasts are small. Lovely, but small. Her waist is small. She has a young woman's hips, legs, and derriere. Her shape is what women call a banana figure. I find her exciting and sensual to look at. Beautiful. She was dressed in a white cotton, short-sleeved top, and faded blue short-shorts that were a bit too tight, and a bit too short, although I had to say, it only made me want to stare.

I suppose it was inevitable. She caught me staring – at least I didn't have my mouth open.

"Oh, Hi! I was just trying to make some peach iced tea. I hope it worked out. Would you like to try some, and be my guinea pig?"

"I promise that if you don't like it, you don't have to drink it," she continued. "Here, try just a taste."

She bent over the table to pour me a glass, and the tight shorts did nothing to hide either her cute behind or the 'intimate area' between her thighs. I caught myself staring and thinking somewhere between, *I shouldn't be looking and she really is beautiful.*

"Oh, I'm sorry," she said, blushing slightly, as she straightened up and turned with a glass of tea with ice.

"It's wash day, and all I had to wear were these old shorts from last year or so. They don't fit, and my mother tells me that isn't exactly my best side."

Your mother couldn't be more wrong, I thought. But acting just like a schoolboy who has seen boobs for the first time in his life, I couldn't get anything coherent to come out of my mouth.

The tea was actually very good, and I told her so – "just like baby bear's porridge, it was 'just right.'" She giggled.

We chatted for a moment, then she said, "Well, I'd better finish the wash."

She picked up the tray with the tea, ice and glasses, and went into the house through the patio door. I found myself staring long after she had entered the house. I'm not sure what I was thinking after she left or whether I could say what was. It was one of those beautiful moments in life that you savor.

Valerie – A Love Story

Dear Diary,

This morning, I saw J out doing some yard work. I squeezed myself into a pair of old shorts – they are way too tight and way too short, and I was afraid I'd pop the button. I took some tea I made yesterday out on the patio. He said hello, and we chatted a bit. I asked him to try my 'experimental' tea and made a show of bending over the tray. I saw him staring. He was so cute. He told me before he thought I was beautiful. I wonder if he still thinks so. When I had my tooth out, he brought me home. I told him I love him. He said he loves me too. Even if he just said it that day because I said it first, it was the most wonderful time in my life. After I gave him the tea, I had to run into the house and change. If mom or dad had caught me in those shorts – outside – I would have been grounded for two weeks.

Ten

The end of the school year arrived. Valerie was thrilled. I hated to admit it, but if she decided to go off to college, I would miss her very much. A day or so after school ended, I saw her in the yard.

"I'm going to miss seeing you go off to school every morning," I said.

"So, you like to watch people go off to spend a miserable day?"

"Well, I didn't think of it that way. I just liked to be able to see you almost every day."

She got that coy look in her eyes and said, "You aren't missing work because you are stalking the neighbor girl, are you?"

"Neighbor woman," I countered, emphasizing the word woman. "And no, I hope that doesn't disappoint, but I'm usually relaxing with a cup of coffee when you leave."

"Oh," she said, sounding disappointed.

"But don't worry, I have altered my schedule a little to make sure I'm having that cup of coffee when you leave."

"I knew it," she said, "stalking. Well, at least I have a stalker. Not everybody can say that."

"Let's hope you only have one," I said.

"I only want one – the one I have, thank you." She smiled, then laughed.

Anna Leigh

Eleven

Some decisions are quick and easy, like what shirt to wear. Some are more involved, like buying a car or a house. We like to think we make decisions based on logic, but in most cases, we use logic to justify the decisions we make on emotional grounds. Here, just hold the puppy.

Summer was passing semi-uneventfully. Valerie spent time researching and visiting colleges. I didn't see her as much as I would have liked. It was a warm, but not hot, evening. I'd thought earlier that the day might be one of the most perfect days I'd seen. I was in the kitchen, sipping a glass of pinot noir, one of my favorites. The sun had just set, and it was turning out to be a beautiful evening.

Valerie appeared at the patio door. She apparently had a pretty good eye to know when Marsha was disappearing for one of her evening events.

Typical Valerie, she looked like she didn't have a care in the world, although she did look a little nervous. "So, I haven't seen you in a few days," she said. "I've been out visiting schools I might attend next fall. A lot of them are very nice. Some are so big, they are scary."

"Going out into the world can be a scary thing," I said. "But college should give you a buffer – a safe place as you move from," I paused, "here, and move into the world. I am going to miss seeing you," I said and tried to smile, but I knew my smile was false. I was going to miss seeing her very, very much.

"I don't mind leaving home," she said, "I'm sort of looking forward to not fixing dinner every night and cleaning everybody's mess in the kitchen. I'll have to study harder, and all that sitting around will probably make me fatter."

"You are not fat," I said.

"Shush! I'm getting to it. The only reason I really don't want to leave is I will miss seeing you every day, too."

"You don't see me every day now," I said, drawing out the word every.

"Do too," she replied. "So, if I were you, I'd realize you have a stalker, as well." She looked pensive, then said, "I wonder if there has ever been a case – before, you know – of two stalkers stalking each other. Huh!"

"What?"

"Yup. I don't hide outside your house, peeping into windows, or anything, but I do manage to see you almost every day."

"I'm going to have to be more careful about what I'm doing."

"And, what you're wearing," she giggled. Then, the smile faded. "But I don't want to not see you every day – or every few days, anyway. I know you think I'm only smitten, infatuated, but I really do care about you and don't want to be separated from you. You probably don't even think about me much. I'm not really all that good looking, and . . ."

"Val – " I managed to get out of my mouth.

She stopped me. "Because I know the other girls at school, and some of the boys, too, think my body doesn't look good."

"Valerie," I finally got out, "I think you are one of the most beautiful young women I have ever met. Your figure is perfect in every way. My only –"

"You're not just saying that, are you?" she asked. "I mean you are so nice, you probably don't want to hurt my feelings. I know I'm just a gawky girl and my body is to big in one place and too little in another place. Plus, I'm just NOT pretty."

"Valerie, every woman in the world seems to focus on things they think aren't right with their bodies. They all think they have to be like runway models – which, by the way, most men don't think are that good looking. You ARE beautiful, and the parts you are probably criticizing are the things that make your beauty unique. I am absolutely amazed at what a beautiful young woman you have become and are. But as I was starting to say, "

"Before you say anything else," she said, "could I tell you a story first? Last summer, a bunch of us girls went on a canoe trip. It was a day long. We had a couple of guides, to show us how to paddle the canoes. We asked the guides how long the trip was going to be, if there would be rapids, all kinds of things. We were all worried about those things, you know, first trip into unknown territory. They told us not to worry about all that. The river was smooth and we should just enjoy the trip, not to worry about how long it would be. So, I spent that day looking through the clear water to the river bottom. I saw fish and logs; turtles, and things. The sun was perfect, and the trees were like a perfect picture. Like the guide said, if I'd thought about how long the trip would be or rapids, or stuff that might be a problem, I never would have enjoyed all the things I saw and felt on that day. All adventures start and end. The best thing to do is enjoy them as they happen. If you worry about everything from how long the journey will last to what might go wrong, and all that, you won't have anything left to just enjoy where you are."

I could only stare as I took in what she had just said.

"Let's go out in the yard," she said. She took me by the hand and pulled me toward the door. I spilled a little of the wine before I could get the glass onto the counter. We walked to an area under a tree toward the back. The moon was coming out from behind a cloud.

"Do me a favor," she said.

"You want my brain for a science project, don't you?"

She hit my chest with enough force maybe to startle, but not crush a bug. "I'm serious," she said.

"I'm sorry," I said. "What is the favor."

"Kiss me. Not like you kiss a little girl, and not like you kiss the little girl next door. Kiss me like you really want to. Kiss me like you really love me. Kiss me like it is the first kiss you ever had and the last kiss you might ever get." While she said this, her face was looking down, her hands playing with her sweater. When she finished, she looked up at me. Her eyes were moving, searching my face, as if she would find her answer there. A slight breeze moved small tufts of her hair. I felt the breeze on my face.

I looked into her eyes and said, "Valerie, I do really love you," and with that I wrapped my arms around her and kissed her as passionately as I could, a kiss more passionate than I had experienced in decades. My mouth moved over hers. We opened our lips and kissed with feeling I couldn't remember. I felt her body against mine, her rapid deep breathing, the movement of her stomach and breasts against me. I felt her arms moving over my back. My heart was pounding in my chest. She pulled her lips away, breathing hard, once, twice, three times, then she crushed her lips against mine. I felt her fingers pressing into my back. I felt her lips, her tongue, her breath, her body. My senses were overloading. Blood was rushing below my waist. I didn't care if she knew or felt it. I don't know how long we kissed; it may have been two minutes or fifteen. It wore us both out.

"Hold me," she said. "I'm not sure my legs are steady anymore." We were both panting.

I wasn't sure mine were, either. I put her arms around my neck and wrapped mine around her waist and pulled her tight against me. A few minutes later, she pulled her arms down between her and me, just wanting to be engulfed.

She whispered, "You really do love me?"

"Valerie," I said and looked into her eyes, "you can fake a lot of things, but you cannot fake a kiss like that.

Yes, I really do love you." At that moment, I realized that in spite of misgivings, fears, and any problems that would come, I had made my decision. There was no going back.

We stood wrapped around each other for a long time.

Twelve

The phone rang three times before she picked it up. "Hello?"

"Hi, Aunt Ruth, it's Valerie."

"Valerie, what a nice surprise. I was just thinking about you. What's up?"

"I needed to talk to someone. My parents would never understand, and you are the only person I can confide in."

"Well," said Ruth, "this sounds serious. Tell me, what has you needing to talk?"

"Aunt Ruth, I think I'm in love."

"You just think you are in love, Valerie?"

"No – I'm in love."

"Well tell me all about it."

"He's the most wonderful," she started but paused.

"Most wonderful what, dear?"

"Well, man," she finished.

"By the use of the word man, Valerie, can I assume he is somewhat older than you are?"

"Yes."

"How much older?"

"Um, I'm not sure for sure. He's not as old as my mom or dad."

"Oh," said Ruth, a bit of concern coming through in her voice. "Has he . . ."

"He's a perfect gentleman. I don't think he would have even kissed me if I hadn't kind of tricked him into it. Well, I didn't really trick him, but I kind of ambushed him. But when he kissed me, my legs got all wobbly and I was really breathing hard. I thought I might pass out."

"Okay," Ruth said slowly. "So, he's older, you ambushed him, and when he kissed you, you almost passed out. Is he in love with you?"

"I don't know," said Valerie. "I hope he is. I don't think he was looking to fall in love – with me, and I know it could be a BIG problem, but I love him so much and I really want him to be in love with me."

"Relationships like this don't always work out, you know. The difference in ages – you will change very much in the next few years. You may drift apart. A lot of things can happen."

"Oh yeah," Valerie began slowly. "There is one other little thing that could be a problem."

"He's married," Ruth finished for her, as she sank into her chair.

"How did you know?" asked Valerie.

"Sweetheart, there were only a very few things that could have been a problem after what you told me. This was the logical one. How did he meet you? Has he done anything?"

"First, Ruth, he lives next door."

Ruth groaned.

"But, I said, he has been the perfect gentleman. I am the one who is stalking him. I've made all the moves. He has said the same things you did a minute ago. But I know he cares about me."

"You know you can trust me," Ruth said. "I won't say anything to anyone," she emphasized the word anyone. "But this could end badly – for everyone."

"I know. He hasn't complained – he doesn't complain about anything, but I know he is very unhappy in his marriage. I think we both need someone. He has helped me with a lot of things and listens when I talk to him. He's not like the boys I've met at school. All they are interested in is gawking at my boobs – or other parts – and making stupid comments. He keeps saying he's too old for me – he's not that old. But I can also tell he feels very much alone."

"Valerie," Ruth continued, "I will support anything you decide to do. Just remember, however, when I say this could end badly for everyone, what I mean is it could be worse than the sinking of the Titanic."

"Thank you, Aunt Ruth. You are very important to me. I need someone I can talk to."

"Just be careful, Valerie. Strong as the human heart is, it can be badly broken very quickly."

Valerie hung up. She was feeling better having talked to her aunt – one of the very few people she trusted. She also trusted and loved Jim, but there are some things in this world you can only discuss with another woman.

Ruth sat back in her chair. She loved Valerie. They used to spend more time together than they did now. She wanted what was best for her, but she didn't know what that might be. Her own husband had been killed in an airplane crash. He was twenty years her senior. It turned heads when they wed, but they had nothing but happiness as long as they were together.

Anna Leigh

Dear Diary,

I went over to J's tonight. I think he was going to say something about us not having a future. I told him a story about our canoe trip and said we don't know how long any trip will be, but we have to enjoy what we have while we have it. I took a chance and asked J to kiss me – really kiss me. I sort of ambushed him. I was afraid he wouldn't, but he did. I almost fainted. I couldn't breathe, but I couldn't stop. My legs started to give out. My body felt electrified. I know all kisses can't be like that – I doubt it, but I will remember that kiss and this night as long as I live. I'll never get to sleep. I'm not sure I want to. This is SO much better than any dream could possibly be. I called Aunt Ruth. She's the only person I can trust with this – I mean I trust Jim, but I needed to talk with someone else. I know Ruth understands.

Thirteen

Valerie came over two days later. She had a folder in her hand.

"I wanted to show you the school I'm thinking of applying to," she started, "but before that, I want to thank you for probably the best night of my life – ever. I couldn't sleep. I thought my heart would explode – and my legs got all wobbly. YOU," she pointed at me, "are a GREAT kisser."

"Thank you," I managed to get out, "you are pretty good yourself."

She continued, "But I do feel a little guilty. It's like I made you kiss me. I sort of trapped you."

"Well, you set the scene," I said, "but I'll take responsibility for my actions."

"So, I'm a responsibility?"

"No, you are a joy. Every time I see you, my heart sings."

She directed her gaze to slightly below my waist, smiled, and said, "That wasn't the only thing 'singing' when we kissed."

I blushed. She giggled. I loved the sound of her giggling. It was sweet, sincere, the sound of true happiness.

Then, we looked at her college choices. She had set aside brochures for all the big schools.

"I decided to spend at least the next year in our community college. That way, I can see if I really like college. If I do, I can transfer to another school – a four-year school – the next year or so."

"I've decided to look at a women's college just across the state line," she said. "I know they have a good business program, and I could even spend a couple semesters in Europe. That would be wonderful. Would that be okay?" She was asking like I would be the one to give her permission for doing what she wanted.

I told her it was wonderful. I would have at least one more year with her before she left for a school farther away. But I was certainly aching, that later she would be so many miles away in school – no more quick visits across the fence – but that she might be an ocean away, too.

But I asked, "So, why there?"

"The community college will allow me to live at home," she said. "Both plus and minus there." "It will be cheaper, for one, and I won't have to put up with all the drama of living on campus. But I will be living at home – with mom and dad. I don't see much changing there. As far as the women's college, I know they have a good program, something I really want, and what I don't want is a bunch of sex-crazed males running after me like Peppy Le'Pew."

"Sounds like you've given it some thought."

"Besides," she continued, "There's only one sex crazed male I'm interested in."

I rolled my eyes, and she slapped me softly on the arm.

"So, do they have night classes?" I asked.

"Why?"

"Well, if they have night classes, you might have to leave for school – to get to your class, of course – before time to fix dinner, and you'd probably return after dinner – and after the kitchen had been cleaned."

"You're devious," she said, "but I love it! There's a little café at school, and I could get something there. That's perfect!"

"I was saving this for last," she said, handing me an envelope. "Don't open it until eight o'clock tonight. Promise?"

"I took the envelope and eyed it suspiciously."

"Promise?"

"I promise." I would have opened it before eight, but I didn't want to have to lie – or tell the truth – if I opened it early. While she might never know, I didn't want to lie to Valerie. So, I waited until 8.

Anna Leigh

Fourteen

The day and early evening passed slowly. I frequently eyed the note with suspicion. Eight o'clock finally came, and I opened the envelope. There was a short note inside. It said, 'Next Friday night at nine o'clock, please sit alone in your study, with the lights off and curtains open. It is a surprise for only you. If your answer is yes, just leave your desk lamp on when you go to bed tonight.'

I was a little curious, okay, a lot curious. At ten o'clock, I turned on my desk lamp, turned off the rest of the lights, closed my study door, and went to bed. Marsha arrived home about eleven.

"Did you mean to leave your light on in your office?" she asked. I was surprised she noticed anything around the house anymore.

"Yes," I said, "I wanted to leave it on. I want the colonists to know the British are coming by land."

"Suit yourself," she huffed. She started to talk about this two-story colonial that she had listed that night. I was staring at the ceiling, a million miles away. A glance toward my office told me that the desk lamp was still on.

Fifteen

The days passed very slowly. And, that Friday dragged. I never thought the time between 8:30 and 9:00 would pass, but finally it did, and I found myself sitting in my dark office just before 9. Not surprisingly, Marsha had another of her meetings.

At 9:03, I started to think either I had gotten the day wrong or she had forgotten or just had something better to do, whatever 'this' was going to be.

But another minute later, the light came on in the room across from my study. The blinds were up, which they hadn't been before, and I realized that my office was directly across from Valerie's bedroom. I felt a little uncomfortable looking into her bedroom from my house. It felt like an invasion of her privacy – even if I was invited – for at least one night.

The room was decorated as I saw when I brought her home from the dental appointment. Pink walls, a few posters. A white poster bed with canopy and a matching white dresser, as well as a small desk. There was a CD player on a nightstand and a TV across from the bed. The My Little Pony had been removed. Her room was neat and clean.

Valerie walked to her desk, picked up her cell phone and punched some numbers into the keypad. She held her phone up and pointed to it. An instant later, my cell vibrated. It was Valerie.

Before I could say anything, she said, "Don't say anything. Just listen."

She pushed a button on her little stereo, and the phone was filled with music I didn't recognize. The music started slowly, and Valerie started to dance – slowly at first, she turned one way then another, her head moving side to side, then around in slow circles. Her arms were making large slow arcs over her head, then to the side. As far as I could tell, her eyes were closed. The music quickened, and so did Valerie's movements, but they were beautifully coordinated, like her dance had been professionally choreographed.

I was almost embarrassed watching, like some sort of voyeur, but I became mesmerized by this beautiful young woman doing a ballet. She was energetic, moving arms, legs, head, torso, everything, smoothly coordinated, moving in perfect time with the music.

Then, as I watched, I realized she was undoing her blouse, which came off as she spun around. Next, were her shorts, sliding down her legs as she bent forward and put her hands on the floor for an instant.

Her bra came off seemingly effortlessly. And there she was, a beautiful nymph, perfectly naked except for a small and very sheer pair of briefs, no sign of embarrassment, doing an energetic, athletic, ballet with me as her audience. She did a pirouette, then another. I don't remember, but I may have had my mouth open. The music and dance went on, and I was entranced.

The song ended – too soon, and Valerie did a final pirouette and stopped dancing. She faced the window and bowed arms out to her sides, as if to thank her audience for watching. When she straightened up, she brought both hands to her lips and blew a double air kiss in my direction. Then, she smiled, cut the connection, and turned off the light.

When the spell was broken, I realized that I was covered in sweat and my shorts were a bit tight. No surprise.

I had witnessed one of the most beautiful and sensual things I had ever seen – I'm not sure I had words to describe what I felt. Excitement, awe, neither were adequate. I took some solace that with her at 19, at least I hadn't been watching a minor.

I put my head back, looked at the ceiling, took a deep breath, and said, "Oh, crap!"

Then, I walked downstairs and poured myself a scotch. My hand trembled as I took my first drink.

After I finished my drink, I sent Valerie a text. 'Thank you. You are beautiful. Your dance was magical.' J

Anna Leigh

Dear Diary,

Tonight, I danced a striptease for J in my room. He was in his office, across the way, so it wasn't like he was actually in my room when I did it. I couldn't see him because his room was dark. It would have been harder if he was 'right there.' I know he saw me because he sent me a text. He said I was beautiful and that my dance was magical. I hope it was. I practiced it before, but I did it with the lights on and the blinds up tonight. I was really, really nervous. I hope he didn't think I was stupid. I shouldn't have done it, and I don't know if I can even say why I felt like I needed to do it, but I did. I know this could be trouble. I hope not. I really, really like him. I know he's married and I shouldn't, but I need to.

Sixteen

Scientists tell us that the brain of a human isn't fully developed until the late 20s, and that teenage emotions run high and strong. Girls' brains supposedly develop and mature sooner than boys. So, boys, it would seem, are more immature and emotion driven than girls – at any age. Of course, the same can be said for many men in their 40s, maybe older, but that is another subject.

I saw Valerie a few days after her revealing dance in her room. It was a Saturday evening and my wife was hosting an open house, miles away. I was in the kitchen, taking a break from a project I had accepted when Valerie knocked at the patio door. She was wearing a pink sweater and blue shorts. Because of the "change" in our relationship, I was both pleased and a little nervous when I saw her.

Typical Valerie, she looked like she didn't have a care in the world, although she, again, did look a little nervous. "So, I haven't seen you in a few days," she said. "And, I was wondering if you thought my little performance was silly. Or if you thought I was too fat or wasn't very pretty."

"You just like to hear me say how beautiful you are," I said. "Your figure is absolutely perfect, and the dance was mesmerizing."

"You don't think it was silly? You liked it?"

"Valerie, while you were dancing, someone could have cut my leg off and I wouldn't have noticed it. And, yes, your figure is perfect."

"You aren't just saying that because you like to look at naked women, are you?"

"You know, you can be quite frustrating at times. You are beautiful."

She said, "I'm glad you think I'm beautiful. I don't think you answered my question about looking at naked women, but that's okay – for now." Then, she kissed me, full on the lips for a good five seconds. I'm not sure I responded. She stopped, stepped back, and with an impish smile on her face said, "Well, kiss me, stupid. You don't expect me to ALL the work, do you?" And I kissed her.

After that first kiss, Valerie and I stayed together for over an hour. We kissed again and again, sometimes forcefully and passionately, sometimes softly and yet, still passionately. While I should have been terrified about what might happen in the future, at least for that time, I was in sheer ecstasy.

Valerie even had me lay on my back on the couch, with my head cradled in her lap. She stroked my hair; I felt her thighs beneath my head and her pink fuzzy sweater on my cheek. I say we were there for over an hour, I'm not really sure how long it was. It didn't seem long enough – just being with her. I say I was in ecstasy, but there were so many emotions, I'm not sure I could describe even half of them. I just know that whatever happened in the future, this moment was worth it. For the first time in years, I was alive.

She finally left, and I missed her as soon as she was gone. And, I knew I was out of control and in trouble. Also knowing how volatile teens can be, I had at least some concern that her attention might turn to anger if she felt neglected or abandoned. Such is the course of forbidden love.

Not that we had done anything really wrong – well, legally, at any rate. I could still very much lose my marriage, friends, work, etc., but I had not done anything that would make me the love interest of the residents of cell block D. While I felt I needed to confide in someone, there wasn't anyone I felt I could turn to.

So, I contented myself with what I had shared with her and hoped the future would provide some way to work it all out. I showered and changed clothes, in the event my wife would even care enough to notice any strange smells. They say a woman doesn't care about a lot of things, but she can spot a blonde hair from across the room and smell another woman's scent from a block away.

When my wife returned from work, she was talking non-stop about the day she had – triumphs and disappointments. She'd stopped with co-workers for a drink on the way home. They'd had noshes with drinks, so she wasn't really interested in eating anything. She went upstairs to the bedroom, went through her nightly ritual, and went to bed early. I headed to the basement gym and did a workout. After dark, I went out onto the patio with a glass of wine and enjoyed the evening, as well as the memory of my unique afternoon.

When I got up in the morning, there was a small bouquet of wildflowers braided together on the fence between our yards.

Valerie – A Love Story

Dear Diary,

Tonight, I spent a couple of hours with J. He said he really liked my dance – the one I did in my room the other night. I was scared he would say he didn't like it, or he thought it was funny. I stayed for a while longer. I sat on the couch and had him lie on his back with his head in my lap. He's so great! He's strong and thoughtful and so many wonderful things. I just loved having his head in my lap like I was there for him for once. He seemed so relaxed and content. I just love him.

Anna Leigh

Seventeen

The office door read, David Anderson, PhD – Clinical Psychology. I had decided I needed to sort some things out. Inside was a desk, a coffee table, a sofa on one side of the table, two club chairs – one on either end of the coffee table, and an Eames chair, done in black leather. The chairs and sofa were done in a mid-gray material. The desk and coffee table were cherry, each with a black slate top. The floor was dark hard wood, with a Persian rug defining the area of the coffee table and chairs. The décor was inviting and at least moderately masculine.

David Anderson appeared to be in his mid-forties. He had brown hair with graying temples. His eyes were brown and soft-looking. He wore a blue shirt under a dark blue sweater vest. Black trousers and loafers completed his look.

He introduced himself as David Anderson, rather than Dr. Anderson, and asked me to take a seat. He took the Eames chair, as I thought he would. I looked at the chairs and couch and tried to decide if there was anything diagnostic about my choice of seat. He must have known what I was thinking, or he must have been asked many times, because after a short pause he said, "There are no right or wrong seat choices." I decided on the couch; toward one end, but not all the way over. That would be like hiding. I hoped it was a right choice.

"Now that we have the important matter taken care of," he began, "would you tell me how I can help you?"

"I'm not sure where to start," I said.

"Well, when I ask people to start at the beginning, some of them say it began when their parents had sex. I don't think we need to go that far back. Why don't you start with either where you want to start, or what you want my help with? I assume you have a problem. I've been in practice a long enough and I have yet to have someone come in and say, 'I wanted to see you because everything is going so well in my life, I can't believe it.' I'll figure out if we have to go back into your past."

"I'm sure you've heard all this before," I said. "I've been married a decade plus. My wife and I married – maybe for the wrong reason – but we were, or seemed, happy. Maybe I just thought we were happy. I don't know. Over the last, well, since we moved here, she has been obsessed with creating a business empire. She sells real estate and wants to be the biggest thing in real estate maybe in the state. I've become a distant second in importance in her life."

"I'm sure that bothers you."

"Yes, well, it does. But there is more. Over the last few months, I have become closer with another woman." I left out any details about who, how old, etc. "So far, we haven't been intimate . . ."

"You mean, had sex," he interjected. "Sometimes you can have an intensely intimate relationship without any physical contact. And that can generate feelings of guilt."

"No, no sex, but this new relationship is, well does feel, more intimate than the one I have with my wife."

"Why is that, do you suppose?"

"Because we are interested in each other. Because when I talk, she listens. She shows she cares. And I care about her. I care about what happens to her. And while this relationship we have probably won't last, I don't want her hurt."

"Is she married?"

"No," I responded quickly.

"She has made no demands?"

"None. She has been supportive."

"Does she know you are married?"

"Yes."

"Do you see her often?"

"Not as often as I would like."

"Okay," he said, "I'd like to ask you about the home you came from – where you grew up."

I made some lame joke about the old "tell me about your childhood" jibe that psychiatrists always seemed to be asking.

"Well, a lot of times – you'd be amazed – the roots of our problems begin early, and it really does help to get an idea about those times."

So, we talked about my home life – growing up in a place where my father and mother were either physically or emotionally absent. I talked about leaving home as soon as I could join the Navy, and while my relationship with my parents was cordial afterward, I rarely went home.

And, we talked about my business for a bit, then went on to Marsha's business and my belief that she wouldn't even be happy when she – if she – built a true empire. Dr. Anderson's manner was casual, but I began to notice he was probing deeply. To my surprise, he asked few questions about "the other woman." He did ask about what we talked about, how she made me feel, whether I could tell how she felt.

The session lasted ninety minutes. At the end, he surprised me. I expected he would want to schedule appointments weekly, or more often, to get to the root of the problem. Instead, . . .

"So, I would say you're frightened."

"Frightened?"

"Well, maybe frightened isn't the precise term. You have a relationship with this other woman that fills a vital need – a hole or void in your soul. Your wife can't or doesn't fill that need – maybe she never did. But as unsatisfying as the relationship with your wife is, it is comfortable – in a sense – and at least safe. The other relationship is attractive – desirable, but it also contains a risk. Your mind constantly fights with itself. Society sees relationships outside of marriage as inappropriate, so you fight with that. Is it moral? Ethical? What are the known and unknown problems if you decide to end your marriage? Some of those are financial, geographical – you'll need a new place to live, and especially emotional. Then too, you may worry whether this new relationship will last or become like the one you have now. What then? What if, when you're free, this woman decides she doesn't really want a full-time partner – that the part-time thing was good for her? All of these things wax and wane, and all of them are scary. As you deal with these thoughts and feelings – and don't minimize the effect of your feelings – you will doubt your strength, the strength of this relationship, and yourself. If there is a significant difference in your age with the other woman, all of this will even be scarier.

It was all I could do to take it all in and not break down.

"Well, Jim," he started. "If you want, we could schedule more appointments, as you work through your issues. I don't usually lay out the problem for a client at the first appointment, but I'm going to do so for you. Whether you stay in a relationship with the woman who is not your wife is secondary. Of course, in my experience, long-term secondary relationships – lasting more than a few months – when a man, or woman, remains married to their spouse – are almost always doomed to failure."

"But your primary issues," he emphasized the word issues, "are first, your reaction to your wife's emotional abandonment of you. It dredges up powerful feelings from your past. That issue is not to be minimized. You were alone, as far as you are concerned, as a child. You are currently alone in the relationship with your wife."

"The second issue is this – if your wife were able to turn it all around, change into a woman who was interested in you, your life, your feelings, your hopes, and your fears, would that be enough at this point, to make you want to stay in the marriage? If she doesn't change, my guess is the marriage will fail – now, or when you become even more miserable."

"I think you are emotionally aware enough to figure those things out without me, but if you want to continue as you work through those things, I'll be happy to help."

I left the office not quite knowing what I was feeling. He had certainly drawn a circle around my problem, but I didn't know if I would have the strength to face it. To do that, I scheduled appointments for the next two months – not long for therapy, but I hoped it would help.

Eighteen

One of my projects had come to the point where it was necessary for me to travel to the West coast for about ten days. While I was happy the project was coming along so well, as a man in love, I was unhappy about having to leave. Valerie wasn't happy, either, but she understood.

The day after I told her I was going to have to leave in a few days, she was at the patio door. "I have a present for you," she said, and handed me a package. Inside was a cell phone. "It is prepaid," she said, "and I'm taking care of the bill. It will always have minutes," she said, "unless you use it to call your other girlfriends. I'll know." She said this with a faux stern manner.

"I could never imagine there could be anyone as wonderful or desirable as," I started.

She cut me off. "I know. Sometimes I just wonder what a wonderful man like you sees in an awkward girl like me."

I just shook my head and said, "Aside from the fact that you are not awkward – you are beautiful, you are caring, intelligent, thoughtful, and you make me feel like everything is right in the world . . . I could turn the tables and ask what a young, beautiful woman like you could possibly see in a man like me."

She laughed. "I guess I'm a little insecure. But I do love you."

"I love you, too. And I'm beginning to think you say some of the things you do just to hear me tell you that you are beautiful."

I left for my trip two days later. I took a cab to the airport; my wife had a meeting, and when I talked about heading out to the coast, she acknowledged it superficially, while checking things on her mobile phone. I didn't necessarily want her to drive me, anyway. Valerie was in school when I left for the airport. I would have liked to have seen her, but that wasn't possible.

I checked in for my flight and boarded the airplane. I was about to turn off my cell phones when the one Valerie had given me buzzed. It was a text – Travel safely. ILY. V. I returned, ILY2. Miss U. J

The days on the West coast went relatively quickly. I was busy, very busy, with the project for about 12 hours a day. After the day, I had a quick meal and retired to my room. There, I prepared for the following day, and about bed time, I would get a quick call from Valerie. She always asked me about my day first, and asked me questions until she had all the details. Then, she would tell me about her day. It was nice – I felt connected and close to her. I'd fall asleep thinking about her and wake in the morning to a text message telling me she loved me and wishing me a 'perfect day.' I usually responded that it couldn't be perfect without her.

Anna Leigh

I tried to call Marsha daily. Mostly, it went to voice mail. Marsha did not respond to my calls, although she did call twice. The first time she wanted to know if I knew where the projector for the laptop was. After that, she regaled me with how she had gotten a meeting with an important client and was going to use it for the presentation. I got a perfunctory inquiry about my project, but before I could give much of an answer, she said she had to go – a call on the other line. The second call was to let me know that she wouldn't be able to pick me up at the airport and I would have to take a taxi. I said I wouldn't mind.

"Okay," she said. "I'll see you at home."

The flight home seemed to take a long time, and as always, the last half-hour of the flight seemed to go on for days. The engines cut back about thirty minutes before landing, the low-powered glide from altitude. Finally, I heard the whirr of the motors extending the flaps, and then the thump of the landing gear extending. The landing was hard, but it was okay. The trip was over and I was happy to be back home. I tried not to ask myself just why I was happy to be home. In my heart of hearts, as they say, I knew.

The weather was overcast. I got off the plane, stopped at the men's room, then went to baggage claim. As usual, baggage seemed to take a long time to arrive. The carousel went around, bags dropped, not mine, and the carousel stopped. Then, it started again. Twice more, the same thing happened. I wondered if it had come on a later plane, or if the ground crew liked 'playing with the passengers' who just wanted to get out of the airport and on their way home. The fourth try was a charm, and my bag finally came around on the carousel. I picked it up and headed for the taxi stand.

There was a limousine driver standing at the exit. He had a sign with my name on it. I figured my wife had a fit of guilt and sent a car, but a limousine? He took my bags and we headed to the curb. He opened the door of a black town car for me and my mouth just about dropped open. Inside, wearing a perfectly tailored women's black suit with a light gray satin blouse, was Valerie. The skirt was cut just above the knee, but in a sitting position, a bit more of her thigh was exposed. She was wearing the slightest bit of makeup; lip gloss, a bit of mascara, and a very light bit of eye shadow.

"Welcome home, sir," she said, trying to sound professional. "I hope you had a pleasant flight."

"Um, thank you." I managed. "Not as pleasant as the arrival. I planned to get a cab."

"No need for that, sir. I'll have the driver drop you at home, and I will continue to the office."

"The office?" I asked.

"Yes sir," she was trying to be professional, but her eyes gave her away. I slid closer and could smell a faint, ethereal fragrance, lavender, either the soap she used, a lotion, or a body powder. One had to be fairly close in order to know the fragrance was there. I moved a bit closer, and she said, "Please, sir. Not in the company car." She was smiling.

"Company car?" I asked. "Um, when did we start doing well enough to have a company limousine?" And to play along I added, "And what department's funds paid for it?"

Again, she tried to look professional, but it wasn't working. "Babysitting," she said and cracked a wide smile.

"You must be babysitting for the Vanderbilts!" But that's the way it was. Every time she would do something extravagant, I'd say she couldn't afford it. Then, she'd tell me that she had babysitting money. She was apparently doing so well at it, I considered giving up consulting and going into babysitting myself.

We managed to hold hands without the driver seeing, and I managed to contain myself, although that task was Herculean. Aside from my surprise – and my joy – at seeing her, I had to wonder whether she was robbing banks or something. Phones, suits, and limousines all cost money, and I didn't know where it was coming from.

I was dropped off in front of the house, and Valerie stayed in the car. It would have been difficult for either of us to explain being together, the limousine, etc. I had to wonder just where "the office" was where she would leave the limo and how she would get back home. But about a half an hour later, she pulled into her drive, wearing jeans, sneakers, and a USC sweatshirt. She was carrying a garment bag that I guessed held her professional garb.

There were two notes on the kitchen counter. The first was from my wife. It was dated this afternoon and said that she had been invited to a last-minute conference in a town about a hundred miles away and that she would be gone for about two days. There was no mention of 'Welcome home,' 'I hope the trip went well,' 'Sorry I'm not there to greet you,' or even a 'Drop dead.' I'd gotten used to that – sort of. Then, I thought of my meeting with David Anderson and out loud said, "No, I haven't 'gotten used' to it."

The second note was from Valerie. It was marked with a later time than my wife's. Her note said, 'I hope you like your airport surprise. It is nice to have you home. I can't wait to see you. I love you.' V

I was mildly concerned about having a note from Valerie on the kitchen counter. If my wife returned, I wasn't sure that I was quite ready for the explosion that would ensue, although I was beginning to believe that Valerie aside, the marriage was not destined to go long-term. Then, too, how did Valerie actually get into the locked house? Oh, well.

I was tired from my trip. The days were getting shorter, and it was dark, and chilly, early.

I unpacked and threw the washable dirty clothes into the laundry and the dry cleaning into the bag to go to the cleaners. I showered and had a bit to eat. Then, I brushed my teeth and poured a glass of wine. There was a knock on the patio door. It was Valerie.

I was thrilled to see her, but I was also dead tired. But I did ask, "How did you get into the locked house?"

Valerie smiled and said, "Your wife came over and wanted to see my parents. She was going out of town for a few days, and in case you didn't get back, she wanted them to have a key to check on things. Well, my parents were out – and will be for two days, so I took the key. Voila. By the way, I made a copy. I hope you don't mind."

I didn't really. I trusted Valerie to use it only when necessary, although I imagined all sorts of scenarios that would result in a catastrophe usually seen only in comedic movies. Of course, those all worked themselves out by the end of the film. I didn't think real life was quite as 'neat.'

Then, she smiled and said, "Since my parents are out of town, do you suppose I could have a glass of wine?"

"Okay," I said. "I shouldn't – only your parents can really give you alcohol – but even then, you can't go out tonight. You need to stay home so you don't get into trouble."

"That shouldn't be a problem," she replied.

Valerie didn't know much about wine, and I didn't want to frighten her with a Bordeaux, so instead, I opened a Vouvray, explaining that it was a light, delicate white wine. I showed her how to taste it and how to sip it.

We talked for about an hour. She wanted to know about my trip and how the project was going. And I wanted to know what she was doing. Finally, the wine was gone and I was tired.

"I need to get some sleep," I said, "but it is really, really great to see you."

"It's really, really great to see you, too." She took off her coat and revealed that she was wearing flannel pajamas. "In fact, I'm going to spend the night with you. We will be fully covered, and since everyone else is out of town, nobody but us will know. So, you go upstairs, and I'll be up in just a few minutes."

My legs were shaking as I climbed the stairs. I got into a set of pajamas, as well, but I knew that avoiding doing something incredibly stupid was going to be very difficult. Well, this was already incredibly stupid, and I knew it, but I didn't care.

When she came up to bed a few minutes later, she said, "Okay. I stayed downstairs for a few minutes so that no matter what, we can say we spent some time together in the evening, then, we parted. And, we'll spend some time together in the morning, but we didn't stay together all night. And, we've got to keep the pajamas on. Okay?"

I ran that through my mind, although I knew the judge wouldn't buy it during the trial I was imagining in my head. *No, your Honor, we didn't spend the night together. I gave her a glass of wine – I know I shouldn't have – and we parted company. I did see her the following morning.* Even I didn't buy it, but I would have agreed to anything at that point with this beautiful young woman in front of me.

I slept on and off that night. I was tired and slept. But I also awoke and marveled at the miracle of this beautiful young woman who had chosen to lay next to me. She actually looked angelic. And the feel of her was heavenly. From time to time, she would snuggle against me, back to me, or front to me, arm or leg over mine. Marsha had stopped doing that sort of thing years ago, and I was amazed at how good it felt and how natural it seemed to be for Valerie.

About 6 o'clock, and before it was truly light, Valerie rolled against me. I was on my back, and she placed her right leg between mine. Her leg was bent at the knee, and her thigh was dangerously close to my growing erection. She opened her eyes and smiled slightly. She kissed my cheek, then kissed me long and passionately on the lips. Her leg rubbed against mine and up a little farther.

Her right hand stroked my stomach and he leg pressed up further. Her hand rubbed over my thighs and started to massage between my legs. That continued not all that long before I exploded.

She continued to kiss and rub until I was reduced to monosyllables. "Wait. Stop. Oh." She apparently didn't understand that continuing stimulation after an orgasm would reduce me to thrashing and semi-convulsing. She giggled and said, "I wonder how long you would keep jumping around if I didn't stop."

"Probably another minute or two when I would die of exhaustion in ecstasy."

She might have laughed or giggled, but she didn't. She smiled, kissed me again, and said, "I thought you might want or need that, even if we aren't undressed. But I'd better go for now. And you'll want to get cleaned up." At that point, she giggled.

She left the room but returned wearing her coat. She had removed her pajama top and tossed it to me. "That has my scent on it. Whenever you want, if you want, you can use it to remember what I smell like. It would be best to keep it where your wife won't find it. A woman can smell another woman's scent a mile away. Trust me."

Then, she blew me a kiss and was gone. I put the pajama top to my nose and inhaled. She was right. It was her scent. And, it was wonderful. Marsha had started to wear perfume a few years ago. I guess she liked it, but I thought it overpowering. I found it somewhat off-putting. *Maybe that's why she wears it*, I thought.

But then, I was sticky and needed to clean up.

I put the top in my office in a safe place. Then, I stripped and showered – and put my night wear into the laundry, which I would do later. I also completely stripped the bed. If women can smell another's scent, the bedclothes would have to be cleaned – or burned.

The sun came up, and it was a beautiful day. The world was not without problems, and I was not without worries, but I enjoyed the day and the memory of the wonderful night I had spent – we had spent.

Anna Leigh

Dear Diary,

I got home today from his trip. I REALLY, REALLY missed him when he was away. His wife is gone for a few days, so I picked him up at the airport. I got a limousine – was he ever surprised. I kind of teased him all the way home. It was actually fun, and I REALLY enjoyed the trip. Later, I went over to his house. He gave me a glass of wine and made me promise not to go out. I surprised him because I had my pj's under my coat. I spent the night with him, although we were both completely dressed. It was so nice being next to him. I wanted the night to last forever. This morning, I started rubbing his legs with mine, and rubbing his stomach and chest. I REALLY loved being next to him and feeling him next to me. I think I must have done something right. He had an orgasm right in my arms! I think I kept it up too long, he was really moving around and made me stop. I left my pj top for him to have. I can't wait to see him again.

Nineteen

I found myself thinking about my life in the days and weeks following the night Valerie and I shared. I truly cared for her and wanted what was best for her. I doubted that would be me. She had her whole life ahead of her and a fair part of mine was gone. I knew that it wouldn't work in the long run and wondered how it might end – especially not wanting to hurt her.

But Valerie had given me something else. I wanted to be a better person because of her. Not necessarily for her, although that was a consideration. I just wanted to be a better person, not someone who was sitting back and watching life roll by.

We had a treadmill in the basement, and I dusted it off and made sure it was working. Then, I started slowly and began increasing time so that I would "run" for about a half-hour per day. I ordered a Bowflex. It came during the day and I had it set up in a few hours. It gave me a way to do resistance training without the danger of dropping weights on myself. Finally, because I was doing the shopping anyway, I started making food choices that were healthier.

Anna Leigh

I found myself dropping a few pounds and moving some weight around to other places, as fat turned to muscle. It wasn't a great change, although I did have to buy some trousers with smaller waist sizes. I also decided to dress better – clean jeans and a shirt instead of grungy shorts and t-shirt. If my wife even noticed, the changes were lost on her. She was busier than ever building her empire.

One day, after my wife had gone to the office, Valerie knocked on the patio door. The weather was now cold, and she was bundled up. I was doing some dishes, and she volunteered to dry while I washed – something of a shock because I'd had no real help with any domestic tasks for at least a decade.

Valerie reached around me to put a dish into the cabinet. She brushed by me and I could feel her arm on my side. Then, she paused and put her hand on my side, then stomach. "Well, someone has been working out," she said with a smile. I blushed. "I hope this doesn't mean you are going out looking for other women," she said with a mock pout.

"You know it isn't," I finally said. "You've just made me want to look better – be better."

"You couldn't look or be any better, as far as I'm concerned," Valerie replied. "You not only look great, you are great. When I've needed someone to talk to about my problems, when I had stupid ideas – why, you've always been there for me. You're not only beautiful on the outside, you are beautiful on the inside, as well."

She kissed me and said, "My birthday is next Sunday. I'll be 20."

"Yes," I said with a smile. "I know it is your birthday, and I know your age. And, while a gentleman should never forget your birthday, a gentleman also never brings up the subject of a lady's age."

"Just checking," she said, also smiling. "Some friends are going out with me. I wish you could be there, too, but I know that can't be. But if you could just send me a text . . . I want to plan something for after that. Maybe we could go someplace nice, like for a weekend?"

Then, she was gone. And things were running through my mind. Yes, we would go somewhere, but if her parents or my wife found out, they would like to string me up.

Anna Leigh

Twenty

Valerie's birthday was sad for me. The weather didn't help. It was cold, dark, and rainy. Valerie meant so much to me and I wasn't able to send her flowers, or even see her. I had bought her a gift. One of those new watches that does everything but exercise for you. I hoped it would be nice enough.

Her parents took her to brunch and her friends had her occupied for the rest of the day. I did send a text – 'Happy b' day. I miss you. I love you.' The 'ILYs' from me were only occasional now. I realized that I wanted her to know that I loved her, and not just send an abbreviation. So, I usually sent, 'I love you.' She must have been sitting on her phone. Almost immediately I received, 'I love you, too. I wish I were there instead of here. I miss you.'

It was four o'clock in the afternoon, two days later when I saw Valerie next. My wife was working at the office – she would probably be there late, putting the finishing touches on another big deal. It was October, and it was getting dark earlier. There was the now familiar knock on the patio door, and my heart rate, as well as my mood, increased. Valerie was wearing a pair of jeans and a soft -

looking white sweater. She had a small paper bag in her hand. She handed it to me.

"It's a piece of my birthday cake," she explained. "You couldn't be there, but I was thinking of you when I blew out the candles. I can't tell you what I wished, though, or I won't get my wish come true."

I said, "Thank you. I was thinking of you, too. And, I wished very much that I could be a part of your birthday celebration."

Valerie said, "It isn't a very big piece, but I thought we might share it, eat it together, kind of celebrating a few days late."

The cake was in a pink box, tied with white string, around all four sides. The string was tied in a bow at the top. Valerie undid the string and peeled back the carton. A modestly-sized piece of yellow cake with white frosting was inside.

Valerie patted the seat of one of the bistro chairs. "Here. Sit." She walked to the drawer where the flat ware was kept and returned with a fork.

She took a small piece from a corner, picked it up and slowly placed it into her mouth. Her lips closed on the fork as she withdrew it. The bit of frosting that was left of the fork was removed – she was licking it with her soft pink tongue. I found myself thinking that I never wanted to be a fork so much in my entire life.

Valerie picked up a second small piece and lifted the fork. It hung in midair for a second, the destination hanging in the balance. Then, she set it back down and said, "You have a little bit of hair out of place." She leaned forward, placing her left hand midway up my thigh. I felt her finger run under my hairline, lifting my hair. Fingers caressed my temple from front to back, then down behind my ear almost to my neck. Valerie sat back, admiring her handiwork.

"There," she said, "better."

I had to agree, although I had shaved and showered earlier and knew nothing was really out of place. Well, nothing except a growing tightness in my jeans.

Up the fork came, and this time, it turned toward my mouth. I was mesmerized. I heard Valerie say, "This will work better if you open your mouth." I did.

The fork slid in carefully. My eyes were locked on hers. They were soft, loving, and energizing, all at the same time. Bedroom eyes. "Now close," she said. I did.

She slid the fork out between my lips, smiled, and said, "See, you're getting the hang of this."

Another small piece of the cake came toward me. I opened my mouth. Valerie leaned forward, her left hand again finding the midpoint of my right thigh. As she sat back to pick up another piece of cake, her hand slid down my thigh. The process repeated, with her hand a little higher on my thigh. My erection was growing, I was starting to breathe more heavily, and I was having some trouble concentrating.

There were only a few small bites left – not that it mattered. Small bites made the cake last that much longer. Valerie slid off her chair and stood on the floor between my knees. Her hips were against my thighs. As she picked up a piece of cake, she leaned forward, my inner thighs and her hips rubbing against each other. Her hand was again on my right thigh – very close to a very noticeable erection. Back and forth, hips rubbing thighs, back and forth, hand rubbing leg, closer and closer. I vaguely didn't want to explode right there, but I was in a place of ecstasy.

There was one piece of cake left – a corner, with a lot of frosting. Valerie picked it up. She put the fork into her mouth, missing slightly, there was frosting on the corner of her lips. She set the fork on the counter and leaned in again. Hips rubbing thighs, her hand now on my erection, massaging. Her lips met mine. I tasted the frosting, and then, her tongue licked between my lips, caressed my teeth, then pushed deeper into my mouth.

My orgasm exploded almost immediately. I was shaking. I couldn't stop. I was mildly embarrassed, but Valerie continued to massage me and wrapped her right arm around me, pulling me tightly against her. She was kissing my neck, then breathing in my ear, saying, "Oh, baby. Yes. Let go, let everything go." I couldn't stop. I don't know how long it lasted. When it finally slowed, I continued to have intermittent aftershocks. Valerie continued to hold me.

Finally, the aftershocks stopped, well, almost stopped, completely. I was panting. Out of breath. I heard Valerie say, "There. That's what I wanted for my birthday. You. Me. I love you."

A breathless 'I love you,' came out of me. When I caught my breath, I looked at her. Soft loving eyes. A perfect smile. A perfect little nose.

Anna Leigh

Valerie held me until I regained a sense of reality. I noticed that in the bottom of the box the cake had come in there was a heart drawn with an arrow through it.

"I hope you liked the cake," she said with a mischievous smile.

"You can bring cake over anytime you want," I said. She giggled. "By the way, I got you a little something for your birthday."

"You didn't need to do that. All I wanted for my birthday was to be with you."

I handed her the box. She unwrapped it slowly.

"Oh, my . . . This is too much. You shouldn't have got . . . Oh!"

I was happy I was able to reduce her to monosyllables for a change.

She put her arms around my neck and squeezed me. Then, she kissed me – hard. "Oh, thank you. This is perfect."

She stayed for a bit longer, admiring my gift. Then, she said she was supposed to be studying, and should get back before her parents got home. She left, and I was left to clean myself up.

I showered and dressed, putting my 'used' clothes into the hamper. It was a good thing that I did the laundry. This would be difficult to explain.

I went to my office. I saw Valerie studying at her desk. I dialed her private line on mine. She picked up her phone off her desk and turned to see me looking at her from my office window.

"Yes?"

"I just wanted to tell you that I love you so very, very much."

"I love you, too." She giggled, "You know, I always heard the way to a man's heart was through his stomach. Your weakness is apparently cake." She was smiling broadly.

"You not only hit the stomach," I started, "but . . ."

"I love you."

"I love you, too."

We hung up. I sat in my office and put on some soft music. There was no way I could concentrate enough to work. I admired Valerie. She was at her desk studying. A better woman than I was a man. Little did I know that Valerie had been staring at the same page for thirty minutes – unable to focus after our little meeting.

Before bed, I went back into my office. Valerie had left her blinds open. A night light showed she was asleep in bed, wrapped around a body pillow. I thought about how it felt to lie next to her, then tried to shake the thought out of my head. I'd never get to sleep.

Twenty-one

The next day Valerie returned. She was wearing a long, warm, dark blue wool coat.

"I wanted to thank you for the wonderful gift. It's perfect."

"If it is perfect, then it is the perfect gift for the perfect woman." I said.

Valerie seemed nervous, and I asked, "Are you okay? You seem to be upset."

"I'm okay." Then, she stood and said "I only have a couple of minutes and have to get back, but I wanted to see you – even if it was only for a short time."

"I love seeing you, even if it is only for a few minutes. And thank you for sharing your birthday, um, cake with me. I wish I could have been there on your day."

"Shush, silly," she said. With that, she unbuttoned her coat. She was wearing nothing underneath. I may have gasped audibly. Not only at the sight of her without anything on, but at her sheer beauty, as well. "I've only got a few minutes, like I said," she told me.

I think I was able to get out an, "Uh huh."

She giggled. Apparently, my complete undoing at seeing her made any of her nervousness disappear. "I didn't think I'd ever have that effect on any man – especially you. So, put your arms around me – inside the coat – and kiss me like you mean it."

And I did. At that moment, I didn't care about anything. I was in heaven and more alive than I had been in years.

"I can see you are somewhat clueless when it comes to this," she said. "So, I guess I need to be the one to take charge. Of course, your ideas matter, but I actually think you like having me in control."

We kissed again. Then, she said, "I want to go somewhere with you for a weekend, or a few days, so that we can do this right. Okay?" I nodded my head in agreement.

With that, I felt her hands on my belt, undoing it before undoing my trousers. The trousers and briefs dropped, or were pushed down on my legs. The erection that had been pushing against them was now free and pushed against Valerie's abdomen. She ran her hands over, under, and around everything private I had. Then, she slowly stroked my erection. It didn't take long for me to erupt – and convulse. I clung to Valerie even more strongly as my body shook. I felt her naked body against mine – hers was soft and perfect. It wasn't a thought. It was spiritual and emotional.

When I finished, Valerie said, "Baby, that was wonderful. I hope you think so, too. I hope this was okay, for you, I mean."

Anna Leigh

"God, I LOVE YOU," I managed to get out, and squeezed her tightly.

"Even if I'm all sticky?" she giggled.

"I love you anyway," I said, "but maybe tonight even more because you are all sticky."

"Okay," she said. "I want to wait for a better time – when you can take your time – for my first time – well, with someone else. But not too long. So, we need to check when we might have a couple of days together. I'll let you know when I can go – actually pretty much anytime in the next few weeks," she gave me a mock stern look as she emphasized the words 'few weeks.' She didn't need to. I was on board.

She pulled out an embroidered handkerchief from her coat pocket and wiped my now very sensitive private area. I convulsed slightly at her touch. Then, she wiped, or tried to wipe a considerable amount of my discharge from her abdomen. I watched, fascinated by her beautiful form and perfect skin.

She folded the handkerchief carefully and put it back into her pocket. "For my trousseau," she said with a smile. Then, she kissed me passionately, took my hand and placed it on her breast. "So you won't forget me after I leave, I hope." *How could I ever?*

She buttoned her coat, kissed me again, and just as she went through the patio door, turned and smiled. For my part, I was left standing by the kitchen counter, pants and briefs around my ankles. Hardly a debonair look, but I didn't care. It had been a surprising and wonderful evening.

Twenty-two

Thanksgiving and Christmas passed pretty much uneventfully that year. Valerie was enrolled in the local community college and was busy with studies. She took my advice and three days a week, her classes convened in the evenings. She was unable to fix dinner or clean the kitchen. She said that made her mother unhappy, but Valerie had told her, "Once I go away to a four-year school, I'm not going to be here, so it will be like easing into it."

We weren't able to see each other on Thanksgiving. On Christmas, about noon, Valerie knocked on the patio door. She kissed me and gave me a small package. Inside was a pair of cuff links, gold, with black studs. On the faces were the symbols of man and woman, entwined. The symbols were inset, gold.

"You can't afford . . ." I started.

"Yes, I can," she said. "I've got babysitting money." Then, she giggled.

"Well," I began, "I'd hoped we'd be able to exchange gifts." I handed her a small package. When she opened it, she found a gold pin, inset with emeralds.

"Oh, my, ... I LOVE this! It is SO beautiful. Oh, thank you!"

"It isn't nearly as beautiful as the woman who will be wearing it," I said.

Now, it was her turn to blush. "I hope you mean me!"

"Yes, of course, YOU."

Valerie kissed me again, then stepped back and looked into my eyes. She was searching my soul, and her eyes held nothing but love. Just the meeting of our eyes was one of the most intimate moments of my life. My heart sang and ached at the same time. She kissed me again, said, "Merry Christmas," then, she was gone.

Twenty-three

Over the years we had been married, I had made numerous attempts to schedule vacations with my wife. Her response was generally along the lines of, "Why do we need to go anywhere when everything we want and need is here."

My response was (also generally), "Don't you feel the need to recreate, recharge, and have time when we are alone together?"

"But we are alone together most of the time," she would reply.

Well, alone. Not together, I thought.

She thought it a waste of time – precious time away from her empire-building. If she gave me a positive response, it would be, "Next year. I just have to (insert whatever you wish here)."

Since our marriage, I've met people who live for their work. Both men and women; they get married because it is expected, or a symbol of "what I'm supposed to do to be a success." Some have children for the same reason. The marriage or children don't represent anything more than a checkbox on the way to whatever goal they think they are pursuing.

I did need to recreate, or as some now write it, re-create. Same word, different emphasis. So, once, twice, or three times a year, I would head off, on my own after asking Marsha once again if she wanted to go. It might be a fishing trip, or hiking in the wilderness. I didn't fish, however. I might want people to think I did. I spent time at a couple of beautiful mountain or coast resorts that cater to fishermen. I might hike, sit on the cabin veranda and read, commune with nature, or just be alone with my thoughts. I'd tip well, spend time in the 'pro shop,' talk with the actual fishermen to see what they were catching, etc. Sometimes I'd even pay for someone's day trip with a guide, if they were nice. It would appear on my credit card statement as 'proof' that I'd gone fishing, not just getting away and relaxing. Why I felt the need to do that, I don't know.

Again, other than a superficial question or two, my wife showed no interest when I returned.

So, it was that in January, I headed to the airport on another recreational outing. Valerie and I had worked out the details of a trip together – well, sort of together. I left out of an airport the next city over, she left out of the one nearby. My flight was the earliest. Both flew to Las Vegas, where we boarded the same airplane for a flight to Santa Barbara. I booked first class seats next to each other, each at different times with different cards.

I dozed a bit on the flight, but I don't think Valerie did. She had flown occasionally, but first class was a new experience, and she wanted to soak it up. I think she was even served a glass of champagne.

Valerie – A Love Story

Santa Barbara's airport is small and quaint. The sun was shining when we left the airplane. The luggage came quickly, and the rental car I had reserved was ready. It was a beautiful California day. We drove along the coast, and Valerie, who had never been to California before, had about a thousand questions, including about the weather.

"The best weather in Southern California is in the winter," I explained. "May and June are usually gray and colder than expected, especially along the coast. So, it is actually strange that this is considered the 'off season.' And, the weather by the coast is cooler than inland. Even in the summer, mornings are cold enough to require extra clothing."

It was the off-season, and I had reserved us a bungalow at a lovely resort on the hills outside of town. We had a beautiful view of the Pacific Ocean. There were a couple of restaurants, and room service was an option, as well, although I didn't want to hide in the room.

It was mid-afternoon when we arrived at the resort. Because it was earlier on the west coast than it was at home, I suggested an early dinner. Sleepy time would come earlier here.

The bungalow had a small living room, a kitchenette of sorts, a bedroom, and two bathrooms – one off the living room, if we wished to entertain. A bouquet of fresh flowers was on the coffee table, and a bowl of fruit and a bottle of champagne were on the bistro table in the kitchenette. There was a welcoming note from the resort manager/owner, Frank Shields, a friend from Navy days, and many days since then.

We had dinner at 5:30 and were almost the only ones in the dining room when we started. We dined until about 7, enjoying a lovely dinner, with champagne, as well as each other's company. We could see the sunset through a large picture window in the dining room.

We walked to the room a short distance away. It was cool after the sun went down, and I put my arm around Valerie, in part to keep her warm, in part to be closer to her. She snuggled against me. In the bungalow, she told me to shower first, "It always takes a lady longer to put herself together," she said. So, I showered, then she took over the bath. And, despite the fact that she was naturally beautiful, it did seem to take a fair amount of time for her to prepare.

Twenty-four

Valerie stood alone in the bathroom, staring at her reflection in the mirror. She had waited a long time for this. She was nervous – very nervous.

"What if I'm not any good?" She asked herself. "What if I do everything wrong, and I ruin the night, the trip, oh my god, what if I ruin the whole relationship because I do everything wrong?!"

Valerie washed, then washed again. She wanted to be clean for this, very clean, maybe cleaner than she had ever been before. She'd never been this close to anyone, she didn't know just what might happen, and she wanted to make sure she was perfect. She'd used her lavender soap. She loved the fragrance, and he told her he did, as well.

She tried to figure out something to do with her hair. No matter what she tried, it just didn't seem to come out right. So, she combed it out as usual and hoped he wouldn't notice. She decided not to put on any makeup. Her hands were trembling and she didn't trust herself to get mascara, lipstick, or eyeshadow on without making herself look like a clown. She hoped he would like her just the way she was.

Anna Leigh

She opted for a pair of sheer panties and a long t-shirt that covered her half-way to her knees, well, almost. Then, she removed the garments and put on a satin night gown she had bought for a "special occasion." She felt weak and shaky as she reached for the doorknob and opened the door.

Twenty-five

She emerged from the bathroom. He thought she was as beautiful as ever, wearing a white satin nightgown. She said, "It is a little long, and it may be a little hard to remove, but I wanted to look nice for you."

"You are beautiful," he said and went to where she was standing. He kissed her and held her. They stood there for some time, kissing and holding each other. Then, he moved her toward the bed. He had a moment of awkwardness and said, "If you aren't sure you . . ." She playfully slapped his chest and said, "I've wanted to be with you – this way – for as long as I can remember."

He pulled back the covers, then moved her to sitting on the bed, then lying down. Valerie felt him kiss her, slowly and softly on the lips. His hands started to move slowly and softly to her body. He lay her head on the pillow. Her hands were feeling his sides, his back. She pulled him toward her. He was wearing only a t-shirt and running shorts. His growing excitement was obvious.

Her hands were trembling and she said, "I'm sorry, I'm a little nervous."

"You don't have to be nervous; I'll make sure you don't have anything to worry about." He realized that he was nervous, as well. Then, he added, "But you can be nervous if you want to be," and he smiled.

He kissed her on the lips, then slowly drew away. He put his hand on the side of her neck, pushed her hair back and he kissed her neck softly. Once, twice, maybe six times. She was beginning to lose count and any desire she had other to enjoy what was happening.

He kissed her shoulders, her arms, then worked his way to her hands, kissing the backs, then the palms. He was able to remove the nightgown without effort. She felt like a rag doll. She was so relaxed that he had to move her limbs for her. She didn't care. She was in a world of complete relaxation and, love.

She felt soft butterfly kisses on her breasts. Her nipples stiffened and she thought, *no one has ever kissed me there before*. "Oooo, it feels so good." Her breath came more quickly and deeply.

His kisses moved onto her stomach and abdomen. Her breath caught. Her heart pounded. Electricity pulsed through her and heat pooled within. Then, he was kissing the tops of her thighs, and she was breathing noticeably heavier and faster. He placed a soft kiss on her most intimate area. She felt a rush of blood and a jolt. She uttered a hushed, "Ooooo," along with a forceful exhalation.

He kept kissing her there, softly, then his tongue was licking her. Her breath now came very quickly and deeply. She thought she might faint; feelings and sensations were flooding her body. She wasn't sure what was happening, but she no longer cared. Feelings, sensations, energy was building up inside her. Was she losing control?

All of a sudden, her back arched, every muscle in her body tensed and stayed tense for what seemed an eternity. Then, she was shaking uncontrollably. Her hands were grabbing the sheets. Her legs were pulling up, her knees in. She was curling into a ball. She exhaled forcefully and continued to shake, and shake. The shaking lasted and lasted. In reality, it was about thirty seconds.

When the shaking finally stopped, Valerie slowly opened her eyes. She was having trouble focusing. She blinked and looked around. She was finally aware of the man with the sand-colored hair who was kissing the inside of her thighs.

"Careful," she said. Slight tremors remained. "I'm really sensitive there right now."

Then, she pulled him up on the bed so she could put her arms around him, kissed him as if they had been apart for months, and said, "Baby, baby, baby. Oh my God. I've never felt anything like that. Oh my God. Oh my God. I love you. I love you. I love you."

They lay in each other's arms for almost a half hour. Then, she rolled over quickly and said, "Wait, you didn't even – you know. You didn't get to . . ."

"I just wanted to make sure that the first time you were with me, it would be all about you. We can take care of the 'other' later."

She hugged him and kissed him again. He could feel her hands on him, working their way down to between his legs – massaging, caressing, and slowly stroking. It didn't take long.

After taking care of the "mess," they lay together in bed, naked, and fell asleep.

Twenty-six

I had two more orgasms that night. I would say we had sex twice, but it was all me. The first happened shortly after midnight. We were in bed, sleeping, wearing nothing. Valerie rolled over and her right arm was on my chest. Her right leg was hooked over mine. She moved her leg up mine and caressed my chest with her hand. It didn't take long for me to respond.

"Oh, my!" Valerie murmured, half asleep. Her leg stayed where it was, and her hand moved down to between my legs. She massaged me playfully. I enjoyed the sensations. Before long, I was breathing harder and "feeling harder." It didn't take very long for me to start shaking.

I got cleaned up and crawled back into bed, where Valerie was already half asleep. She welcomed me back with a soft kiss, then rolled onto her side and wished me "Sweet dreams." They were.

Sometime later, it was still dark, she moved backward against me, her cute bare derriere pressed against me. All she had to do was wiggle a bit, and I was once again, "growing." It didn't take long for Valerie to awaken, at least part way.

"Oh!" she exclaimed. "Your little friend seems to be very persistent," she said playfully. Then, "I suppose we need to take care of 'him' so we can get some sleep." She started to massage and stroke me once again. "You keep telling me you're an 'old man,' but I would never have been able to keep up with you if you were my age." It took a little longer this time, but Valerie produced a third orgasm for me in less than four hours. She gave me a kiss and a smile, then said, "Maybe I should consider a leash – either for you or," she paused, "him," pointing down at my now soft member.

The rest of the night went without further interruption. While I was somewhat embarrassed, I realized it had been a LONG time since I had been able to perform 'thrice' in one night. However, there was still the actual act of intercourse that remained. I worried that it would be painful for her and I didn't want to hurt her.

We were up earlier than I thought we would be. The sun was just hitting the ocean, which was still flat from the night before. The little bit of fog was disappearing quickly. I showered and dressed. Valerie took a bit longer – she told me a woman just takes longer to 'prepare.' It took all of fifteen minutes. There were occasions when my wife had taken three hours and didn't look as good. Valerie wore jeans and a resort sweatshirt she picked up the day before. We walked to the dining room. We were one of three couples. We had a large breakfast, along with a couple of mimosas. The wait staff might have been skeptical, but they served us – both.

We went back to the bungalow and spent more than an hour sitting on the porch and talking. She asked about my current project and listened intently as I answered. She asked questions that showed she understood what I was doing and was interested. I asked about her plans. She thought about studying international business practices. I have to admit, while I found her charming, engaging, and interesting, and I wanted what was best for her, I felt a sense of loss just hearing about her going away to school, where our frequent, short meetings would be a thing of the past. I tried my best to put those aside.

After our chat, we hiked the hills around the resort, and toured the small winery kept on the premises, just to show how wine is made. Of course, we bought a couple of bottles of the resort wine. We had a small lunch at the dining room, then we drove to the beach and strolled along the sand, watched the ocean waves break, and talked some more. I bought a bottle of champagne and orange juice, along with a few other things, at a grocery store. It was a lovely day.

We had a light dinner at a small café on the beach. It was relatively early, and we returned to the resort, and our bungalow, in time to make mimosas and watch the sun set. It was another beautiful California sunset and I enjoyed sharing it with Valerie. It was one of life's perfect moments.

Twenty-seven

After the sunset, we went inside. Valerie emerged from the bath wearing a long t-shirt. She had spent a fair amount of time – for her – making sure she was once again, 'presentable.' She saw him standing near the fireplace. He was wearing only a pair of running shorts.

She went to him and put the side of her face against his chest. He kissed the top of her head. She turned and kissed his chest. His skin was warm. He held her in his arms. Her arms were pulled against her body, folded against her upper body. She delighted in being cocooned by him.

He lifted her chin and kissed her – a long, soft, passionate kiss. She put her arms around his neck. Then, she felt him lift her off her feet. He carried her to the bed and lay her carefully on her back. As before, he started to massage her, softly at first, more deeply as she relaxed.

He slid the briefs she was wearing off her hips and down her legs, planting butterfly kisses on her legs as he did so. Then, he continued with the massage, adding kisses to relax her. She sat up to kiss him, and as she did, together they removed her t-shirt. She felt as if she were in a slow-motion dream.

She lay back on the pillow and in spite of herself, closed her eyes as she immersed herself in the feeling of the massage and light kisses on her body. He kissed both her palms, then carefully set her arms on the bed, moving to her neck. Kisses rained on her neck, then shoulders and chest. The delightful feeling of his lips softly kissing her breasts made her nipples stiffen.

"God," she said softly, "I've never been so relaxed. I feel like a jellyfish. I'm floating."

He continued kissing her and she felt his lips travelling slowly down her stomach to her abdomen, then legs. Her mind was wild with anticipation. At last, she felt his soft kiss between her legs. She uttered a soft, "Ohhhhh," and enjoyed the sensation. She felt the sensations she experienced yesterday starting to build again. Again, there was a sense of rushing energy. She was breathing hard and she could feel her heart pounding.

She felt him move up her body. His face was over hers. Then, she felt him start to enter her. At first, he only just touched her, then, he inserted himself, but only the tiniest bit. He withdrew, only to reenter, just a little bit further. With each thrust, Valerie was breathing harder.

Each thrust was just a bit deeper. Valerie somehow thought, *Oh, my God, he's teasing me!* The slow, ever deeper thrusts continued until Valerie felt something, she wasn't sure what. She didn't care. She was past caring.

Valerie grabbed his body and pulled. She wanted to have him all. With that, he pushed forward all the way, fully inside her. She lost her breath at the sensation. Then, all she knew is that they were moving together, he was thrusting harder and harder. She couldn't get enough. She pulled him and kissed his neck, his chest, his mouth.

Valerie felt all the energy in her body explode in an orgasm. Her arched back lifted them both off the bed. Her eyes were closed, as she exhaled forcefully, she made some noise, she wasn't sure what it was. As she started to shake, she felt him start to shake and convulse, as well. Each time she would shake, he would shake more. Each time he shook, she would start again.

She didn't know how long it lasted. They finally collapsed, side by side, panting, trying to catch their breath.

Twenty-eight

It took Valerie a full five minutes to recover before she said anything. She rolled over, hugged me, kissed me, and said, "Oh my god! That was SO WORTH waiting for!" Then, we both laughed. "I never dreamed it could be like that!" I explained that she had inspired me. Then, she laughed and said, "I loved it, but I hope you aren't going to be 'inspired' twice more tonight. I might not live through it."

We lay there for a few minutes. I rolled on my side and asked, "Are you okay?"

"Okay? I've never been so okay. I've heard other girls say that the first time is painful, so I was a little worried about that. But by the time we got to 'that part,' I was so relaxed and excited, all I wanted was to have you deeper and deeper. I felt something, but it didn't matter. You were wonderful."

So, I was wonderful. I didn't think I was, but I felt good that relaxing her completely, then making sure she was 'half-way there' before I tried to enter her had worked. I was somewhat surprised that I was her first. I knew there were at least a hundred guys who could have 'come' before me – and would have if it had been up to them. But

Valerie had given me that privilege. And, because we had had our orgasms together, extending the sensation – and the thrashing around, Valerie referred to this as the Great California Earthquake.

We actually had one more 'inspiration' that night. This one was completely Valerie's, well, mostly Valerie's 'fault.' We were in bed, naked, and she rolled over to me and said, "One more time tonight, please." How could I refuse? I reached for my condoms, and she told me that they weren't necessary. "I started on BCPs a month ago," she said. Still, I put one on. I wanted to give the pills more than a month, but I had another reason, as well. Condoms help decrease stimulation and made it possible for me to last a little longer.

The second time was shorter, less involved. I explained that beforehand, which Valerie understood. The condom allowed me to last longer than the average teenager having sex for the first time. I thought it was a good thing Valerie wasn't experienced. If she were, she'd know that I was certainly nothing special.

The second time was it for the night. We both fell asleep and slept well until sun-up.

The following morning, we both showered and dressed, then went to the dining room for breakfast. Again, it was larger than what I usually had, but I was feeling great, and I was enjoying myself.

In the late morning, we went to the harbor, and I rented a twenty-five-foot sloop. The wind was coming up, and we would be able to sail around the harbor a bit. I stayed inside the harbor. I didn't know how much time Valerie had spent on the water, and I didn't want to have her get sea sick out on the ocean, where the wind was making the waves higher and choppier. We spent about three hours sailing around, then came back in and had lunch at a small restaurant on the harbor.

It was mid-afternoon by the time we got back to the bungalow. The resort had a small putting green and putters. We played with those for a few minutes. There was a small field and a soccer ball nearby. Valerie said, "Neat." She wanted me to stand about twenty-five feet away and place my hands over my stomach and chest, like I was going to catch a football.

She said, "Just stay there, I'll kick it between your arms. You can catch it."

Remembering the girl who couldn't keep the ball in her own back yard, I was a bit more than skeptical.

"Don't panic," she said. "I can do it."

I wasn't panicking but I might have been close, fearing possible disfigurement – IF she was off, but not enough to miss me completely.

She stepped back at a forty-five-degree angle, looked at me once, then concentrated on the ball. Two steps and she launched the ball with amazing speed and grace. It landed exactly between my arms and almost knocked the breath out of me.

"When did you learn to do that?" I asked.

"I was high scorer for my team, three years running."

"So, how come you couldn't even keep it in your own back yard?"

"Well," she said, "I could, but at first, I just wanted to say 'Hi!' and that seemed like a good way to break the ice. You were so nice; I'd lob it over when I wanted to talk. I just couldn't do it very often, or you would have figured it out. Later, I lobbed it near your far fence 'cuz I wanted to see you bend over to pick it up. You have a cute butt, by the way."

I blushed. "I might have just kicked it back over."

"Nope," she said, "I saw you try. You can't kick to save your life. And, I got to see your cute butt. By the way," she continued, "you've been working out. I noticed that before this trip."

I had to laugh at the way Valerie had been so clever to work her plan.

"Has she noticed?" Valerie emphasized the word 'she.'

"Um, no."

"That's because she doesn't look – or touch. While I never planned to have an intimate relationship with a mature, married man, you were just so wonderful to me. And I know you were missing something - someone in your life. Like me. I guess it – we – just evolved."

"But as long as I'm being honest, do you remember the day I was making the tea?"

"Oh, yes, I remember," I answered. I drew out the word 'yes.'

"Well, I really wanted to talk to you. Mom was shopping and dad was playing golf. I grabbed some peach iced tea we had and got some ice. I also wanted to know if you thought I was worth looking at, so as fast as I could, I

Valerie – A Love Story

squeezed myself into an old pair of shorts that were WAY too short and WAY too tight. Then, I saw you looking at me when I bent over to get the tea."

By now, I was really laughing at the way I had been 'played.'

"So, what were you thinking?" she asked.

"At first, I was thinking that I shouldn't be looking, you being a young lady – too young a lady. But you caught me looking at your lovely . . . um, anatomy. Then, you apologized for the old shorts – laundry day or something – and told me that your mother didn't think that was your best side. I caught myself thinking that your mother couldn't be more wrong."

Valerie giggled. "Right after, I had to run into the house and change out of those shorts. If my mom had caught me talking to you and wearing them, I would have been grounded for a month."

I laughed again, but I couldn't help thinking I was on a trip – an intimate trip – with a young woman whose punishment was still 'being grounded.' We went inside and started a fire in the fireplace. I opened a bottle of wine and we sat on the sofa talking.

After about a half hour, she jumped from where she was sitting and landed on top of me. She started tickling and wrestling with me, which shortly turned into more sensuous wrestling, less tickling, and more kissing.

She started unbuttoning my shirt, then belt, saying, "This time, I want to try being on top – okay?"

She won the wrestling match, and the undressing contest, if it was actually a contest, and sat with her legs on each side of mine. She wanted to know what to do next. I told her, and she did it to perfection. Watching her and feeling her move on top of me was pure poetry in motion. As our time in the resort had lengthened, so had my time in achieving orgasm – more to me wearing out than to any prowess. When I finished, we were both panting hard.

"I must not have been any good," she said. "It took you a long time."

"You did great," I replied. "I'm not used to 'performing' at this level and frequency, and it just takes longer each time."

I helped her climax, then we headed to the shower.

Dinner was light, followed by an early bedtime.

Twenty-nine

It was early afternoon; our last full day in Santa Barbara. Valerie and I had spent the morning walking the beach. We'd crossed over to look at souvenirs in a small shop. Valerie wanted to go back over to the beach, so we walked to a crosswalk. Something caught my eye, and Valerie started across before I did. She was about halfway across the street when I saw movement down the street. A silver car had turned the corner and was heading our way. The woman behind the wheel was on a cell phone and wasn't paying full attention to her driving.

I started to call out. "Val," was about all I got out. Valerie was turning toward me, but she was turning the wrong way and she wouldn't see the oncoming car. I was leaning forward, starting to move and pushing as hard as I could with my legs. The car was getting dangerously close, and I didn't think I'd make it. I launched myself as hard as I could, outstretching my arms.

My hands connected with Valerie's stomach while I was in mid-flight. She started to move backward from the push. Her arms came up from her sides as she tried to balance herself. I saw her legs start to back pedal to keep her from falling as her body began to move backward.

Somewhere in my brain, I realized she was now out of the car's path.

Then, I felt a strong force hit me along the left side of my body. I flew up, and started rotating. I saw the sky for an instant. Everything was moving as if in slow motion. Then, I landed – hard – on my left side, my arm was under my head, keeping it from hitting the asphalt. Slow motion stopped and everything returned to reality. I completed the roll and stopped on my back.

Someone yelled, "Stop the car! Stop the car!" and I heard tires squeal.

A woman yelled, "I think I hit someone, I'll have to call you back."

I remember the blue sky, and the sun hitting my face. Then, Valerie was there. "Oh my god! Oh my god! Oh my god! Oh my god!" Her hands were over her mouth and nose.

I reached toward Valerie with my left hand. "Are you okay?" I asked. She stared. Later, she said she couldn't believe that I was asking if *she* was okay. I asked again, "Are you okay?" She nodded her head.

A policeman wearing a blue and white helmet came into view. A gold badge was emblazoned on the front of the helmet. He was wearing sunglasses. He was upside down. "How many fingers am I holding up?" he asked. I couldn't quite figure out why that was important. I wanted to know that Valerie was alright. I'd been hit by a car, and he wanted me to count fingers.

"How many fingers am I holding up?" he asked a second time.

I figured that I could give stupid answers to stupid questions. "I've never been good at math," I replied.

"How many fingers am I holding up?" he asked for a third time. "It is important."

I counted three. "Three," I said, hoping he wasn't hiding a fourth somewhere I hadn't seen.

"What is your name?

I told him.

"Try not to move. Do you feel any pain?"

"I think I'm okay." I started to move my fingers, then my toes. Everything worked. So far, so good. I opened and closed my fists. I rotated my hands and feet. Valerie was crying. I slowly moved my forearms, then my arms. The police officer tried to get me to lie still, but I told him I needed to take inventory. My legs seemed to move okay.

"We've got an ambulance on the way. You need to be checked at the hospital."

The officer looked at Valerie. "Are you his daughter? You can ride in the ambulance if you're his daughter."

"I'm going in the ambulance," she answered.

I don't remember much about the ride to the hospital. Valerie held my hand. The EMT took vitals after starting an IV. The ambulance crew took me into the ER, where they removed my clothes. It took only a 'short' four hours for them to do enough x-rays to worry me about radiation exposure. They sucked blood, took urine and did neurologic exams. After four hours they said I was very lucky. I didn't seem to have any major injuries. I would, however, be very sore and have some bruises. They said they would like to keep me in the hospital overnight for observation.

I told them that I'd be more comfortable at the resort, and since Valerie was a nursing student, she could keep an eye on me and let them know if anything bad started to happen.

The police officer arrived to take our statements. Valerie gave her real name and address. The police officer asked, "I thought he was your father?"

Valerie said, "He's not my biologic father." I made a note to myself that she was very clever and that I shouldn't ever try to outsmart her.

Finally, I got dressed. The nurse came in with discharge instructions and a list of tasks for my daughter, the nursing student. The nurse looked to be about 50. She was nice looking, but she had also seen a lot in her life. You could see it in her eyes. Valerie was lost when it came to the instructions, but I made an "OK" sign with my hand, and Valerie just played along.

The nurse had Valerie wait outside while she got me into a wheel chair. She looked at me and said, "Not my biologic father. Romance. If I weren't a hopeless romantic, I'd turn you both in. Try not to get yourself killed. Okay?"

"What gave us away?" I asked.

"I may have been born in the morning," she quipped, "but it wasn't yesterday morning. First, the way she looks at you. Unless you have something going on with your stepdaughter," she drew out the word stepdaughter for about five seconds, "that I don't want to know about, her eyes are a dead giveaway. Then, she wouldn't know a syringe from an autoclave. And, from personal experience, it isn't your body that worries me – you're strong as an ox – I'd hate to see a broken heart – for either of you. Take it from me, love is . . ." she stopped there. "Trust me. If a guy ever jumped in front of a car for me . . . And that's why I'm not turning you in."

Thirty

We took a cab back to the resort. Valerie wanted to help me into the room, but I made it, well, most of the way, under my own power. I said I was starving, and she called down for room service. Somehow, she told them what had happened.

Before the meal arrived, there was a knock on the bungalow door. It was Frank Shields, the owner/manager. He came to check up on me. When he saw that I seemed to be okay, he couldn't help giving me a hard time.

"You should learn to walk in the crosswalks," he started.

"I was in the crosswalk – well, at least at the beginning. It wasn't my fault somebody moved me out of the crosswalk."

"You didn't look both ways, did you?" he kept on.

It was actually true; I hadn't looked both ways. All I remember seeing was the car heading for Valerie. I started to sweat, thinking I might have actually pushed her in front of a car coming the other way. "Oh, God," I said. "I might have . . ."

"But you didn't. You did manage to get yourself hit, however."

We chatted a bit longer, then dinner arrived. Frank went to the door. Valerie went with him and stepped out onto the porch. Before the door closed, I asked if Frank could send us a blood pressure cuff and thermometer – I stressed an oral thermometer.

"You're his friend, aren't you?" she asked.

"I've known him since the Navy. We were on the same ship together."

"The one with the fire?" she asked.

"Yes, the one with the fire. So, he told you that story, did he? He must trust you very much to tell you about that. I don't suppose he told you that he was the only one to actually look at the men who were killed. After he went in, the bodies were covered with sheets. Investigators came on board, removed the bodies for autopsy, and did a thorough investigation. Nobody else from our crew ever saw their friends and shipmates – in that condition."

"What condition?" she asked.

"They were burned – badly."

Valerie only got out a quiet "Oh."

"He didn't tell you any other stories?"

"No. He just seemed ashamed of what he did then. He's only human."

"I'm not quite sure of that," said Frank. "I was a young seaman. Well, we were all young. I was working in the engine room. Something was wrong with one of the large pieces of machinery. I was sent in to take a look, and I mean *inside* to take a look. Inside the machine. My leg got trapped in some gears when they moved. If the gears had turned any more, my leg would have been crushed, then" – he paused – "removed. By the machine."

Valerie gasped, "Oh, no."

Frank continued. "They had to take the machine apart, but it could have moved at any time, and I would have been killed. The guy in there who doesn't think he has ever done anything brave crawled inside the machine with me. It was dark, cold, and I was scared to death. He brought me something to eat and drink and stayed with me the six hours it took to disassemble the machine. He would have been killed, too. When I was really scared, he said, 'Look, killing one sailor would be terrible, but if the skipper let both of us die, his career would be over.' We both laughed so hard the rest of the crew wondered what we were talking about."

"He had them take me out first. He came out after me. I owe him my life – at the very least, my sanity."

"Ask him about the time we were in the Philippines," Frank continued. "A lot of rain. Floods. Swollen, raging rivers. He went in with a rope tied around his waist to rescue a woman and her two kids. Damn near drowned. The only thing the rope would have done was to help retrieve the body."

"So, you make sure you take good care of him."

Thirty-one

We had our dinner. I asked what she and Frank had talked about.

"He said you saved his life."

"Not true," I answered. "I just kept him company while the crew saved his life."

"And, you could have been killed if anything had gone wrong."

"Well," I said, "I didn't say there wasn't a possible downside."

She hit my arm playfully.

"Then, he said you went swimming in a raging river to save a woman and her two children."

"She owed me three dollars – American. Besides, I'm not sure the river was 'raging' – a bit high, perhaps. You should really watch out for Frank. I think senility is creeping in early. He tends to exaggerate."

She stared at me. "I can't believe it. You just won't admit you are a hero."

"I'm not a hero," I said, "just an ordinary guy who sometimes finds himself in places where things need to be done. It's really kind of my bad luck."

"Nope," she said. "Hero. Hero. Hero."

We finished dinner. There was a knock on the door, and the medical supplies arrived. I showed Valerie how to take a blood pressure and pulse. She already knew how to take a temperature. Just to be cute, Frank sent over both oral and rectal thermometers. "Just in case," the note read.

"Just in case of what?" asked Valerie.

"Just in case you feel the need to embarrass me," I answered. She rolled her eyes.

I told her she should take my blood pressure, pulse, respirations and temperature about every hour – and write them down. She did it dutifully while I watched.

Thirty-two

Valerie put the medical stuff on the dresser, then came back to the bed. She knelt next to me, wearing a t-shirt and running shorts. She started crying.

"Why are you crying?" I asked.

"You could have been killed!" she said. "What were you thinking?"

"Well, if I would have had a lot of time, I might have thought, 'There's a car coming and it's headed for Valerie. I've got to do something.' I don't think I thought. I reacted. I HAD to get you out of the way of that car." I tried to be cute. "I hope I didn't make you hurt your cute little . . ."

"But you were hit!" she said. "You could have been killed." Great big tears were rolling down her cheeks and landing on her t-shirt and legs.

"Well," again I tried to lighten the mood, "no plan is perfect. Each has its weak points."

"Stop it!" she said. "I don't want you to be funny. What would I do if – if . . .? I couldn't . . . It was so close." She was sobbing.

Anna Leigh

I told her to come to me. She said I was injured and needed rest. I told her she needed to be held, that I was fine.

"You could have been killed," She said.

"I can think of no better way to die than saving the woman you love." It sounded a bit hokey, but I meant it.

"Loved. It would have been loved. I would have been left visiting a grave every week, bringing you flowers and telling you the latest news."

"Love. I will love you forever. I mean that."

Valerie came over to my side. She put her head on my chest and her right hand on my stomach. She was curled into a little ball. After a bit, her crying stopped. "I can't believe I almost lost you," she murmured.

An hour or two later, I awoke to find that Valerie had moved about a foot away from me. Her hand was on my side, as if she was afraid that if she let go, I might disappear. Her hand stayed on me all night as I drifted in and out of sleep.

Thirty-three

The next morning, I awoke to a bright sun shine day. I looked at the readings Valerie had taken. They were done every hour on the hour. She had done it without waking me. *She should teach nursing,* I thought. I had her call the ER and speak with the nurse – our nurse. I told her what to say so she would sound professional. When she hung up the phone, she had a smile on her face.

"What's so funny?" I asked.

"The nurse you had yesterday? The one who got you into the wheel chair?"

"Yes?"

"Before she hung up, she just said, 'Tell your, um, patient, I wish him the best. And oh yes, try not to wear him out.' She also said to not let you play in the street anymore. Do you think she suspects?"

"Oh, yes. But I think we found a hopeless romantic who wants a happy ending to every story. She rarely sees them."

Thirty-four

Our flights back home were later in the day. We enjoyed a romantic interlude before having a great breakfast, I felt pretty good and wasn't too terribly sore from my adventure the day before. Valerie was a little leery about 'physical activity,' but I convinced her that I was feeling fine, even if one side of my body was a bit bruised and dented. She was gentle, and everything went well until I climaxed, when I discovered where all the sore parts really were. Afterward, we lay in each other's arms. I think we both wanted to stay there forever. Valerie chided me for trying to perform during the time I was an 'invalid.' I told her I took offense. She said, "Good."

I had stayed at the resort many times before, it was one of my favorites, although this was the first time I had ever had a companion. I'd suggested Frank's resort to others who stayed there when they were coming to the area, and increased his bottom line. Aside from that, I didn't stay there "on the cheap," and he appreciated my business and over-tipping. He had a moment to chat.

"Frank," I said, "the place looks great, as always. And your staff has been, again, superb."

"They always appreciate serving a gentleman, and someone who appreciates them. You have always been a most gracious guest. You feeling okay?"

"Yes, thank you," I answered. "First things first." I handed him an envelope with a rather large gratuity. He told me it was not necessary, as they were always happy to have me stay.

"Second, I'd like to ask a favor – no obligation to do so, and it won't change my behavior, my recommendations, or the frequency with which I stay."

Frank sensed where I might be going. He said, "Whenever you wish to stay again, just give me a call personally when you know you will be here. The bungalow for one person will be ready then, just as it was on this trip." I thanked him profusely. We shared a glass of wine. As I left his office, Frank shook my hand. He said, "Good luck. I can see you two really care for each other. If it ever comes to that, I'll be hurt if I'm not invited." I headed back to the bungalow to pick up Valerie and my small bag.

Security at the airport was tight. They aren't making any mistakes in Santa Barbara. Before we knew it, we were on the airplane and headed back to Las Vegas, where the plan was for us each to take a different flight with a different routing, in case we were spotted arriving home. But I couldn't quite stand to leave her in Las Vegas, so we checked the flights. Mine had an extra seat in first class, so I bought a ticket, and we rode the final legs together.

It was dark when the plane landed. I had Valerie leave first and pick up her luggage. When she was headed to the taxi line, she sent a text, and I left the arrival concourse and headed for home.

Even though it was late, there was a note on the kitchen counter. Since I wasn't going to be home until late, Marsha had decided to go out to dinner with friends. While I didn't really deserve it anyway, I noted there was no 'Welcome Home' or anything like it on the note. It wasn't even signed.

I took my carry-on bag and headed for the stairs when there was a tapping on the patio door. I knew who it was from the sound of the tapping. Valerie was there.

She said, "I could tell she wasn't here because the house was dark when I got home. I just wanted to say 'good night' and thank you for the most wonderful four days of my life." She kissed me passionately, and I returned her passion. Once again, it resulted in a 'lower enlargement.'

"Later," she said. "We can't take the chance that she will arrive home while we are in the middle. I promise it won't be long," she giggled, "the TIME won't be long, but I know it will seem like forever for both of us."

We kissed again. Then, she was gone. I went to my study. Her curtains were open. She blew me a kiss, then she undressed slowly and seductively. I groaned. I turned on a small light that barely illuminated the room. It was enough for me to be seen by her. I blew her a kiss, as well, then picked up my 'private' cell phone and sent 'I LOVE YOU.'

I put my clothes into the wash, took a shower, then went to bed, thinking about a wonderful few days I had experienced. Marsha came home about an hour later.

Valerie – A Love Story

She quietly put on her pajamas and slid into bed. Neither of us said anything.

I was up about an hour before my wife. She came downstairs, looking a little 'rough' as they say, searching for coffee. I poured her a cup and said good morning. She took a seat on the far side of the table from me.

I asked her about dinner. "We ate with the Caldwell's – Bill and I. You know Bill – from the agency." I knew Bill. "We had dinner at Chez Marquez. The service was slow, and the food so-so. I was almost embarrassed. We're trying to land this big account, and we end up in a place with slow service and food more expensive – by far – than it should be. Still, we think we may be able to convince them to use our services for their retail purchase. Maybe retail purchases." She emphasized the plural. Then she said, "California?" She said it as though she felt obligated to ask, but really didn't want to know any details.

"I had a great time," I said. *Truly, not a lie.* "I did some hiking" *true,* "sailing" *true,* "wine tasting" *true,* "and spent a fair amount of time laying around" *true, but not the entire truth.* I would have elaborated, leaving out the part about why the trip was so great, but there wasn't any interest.

"It is a great place. Great weather, lots of activities. We should go – you and I."

"Okay. I'll give it some thought. Probably not until next year. There are some major things coming up." She was looking at the paper.

I figured I had to give it a chance. If she would have said, "Yes! Let's go right now!" I'm not sure I know how I would have felt. And maybe I asked knowing what her response would be. But it was always the same reply, "Maybe next year."

She showered, put herself together, and was off. I sat thinking about Valerie and California, and what might have been some of the best days of my life.

Thirty-five

The weather was warm. It was a lovely night, about 8 o'clock. There was no moon. The night was very dark. The temperature was in the upper 70s, and there was almost no real wind, maybe a slight breeze.

I was sipping a glass of wine in the kitchen, a Riesling I particularly liked. There was the familiar tapping on the patio door. "Is she home?" asked Valerie. She was wearing a long robe and tennies.

"No. She had another client meeting and open house." My wife liked evening open houses. She said more people could come, and she usually put on a small spread. It seemed like seeding grain on a field to bait the animals you were hunting – a practice outlawed in most states – but I guess the law thought humans were smarter. They aren't.

"I didn't think so," said Valerie. "I saw her go out with her usual work stuff. Come on." Valerie started to pull me out the back door. I put the wine glass down on the counter.

"Where are we going?" I asked.

"You'll see," she answered.

Anna Leigh

Valerie pulled me to a relatively secluded corner of my back yard. She started kissing and nuzzling my neck. And she started whispering into my ear how much she loved me.

"What . . ." I started to ask as I felt her starting to undo my belt.

"Shhhhhh!" she whispered.

"We can't just . . ." again, I started.

"We can if you don't make too much noise," she said. By then, the belt was undone and she was making quick work of the trouser button and zipper. They dropped to my ankles. She pushed my briefs down, as well. Her hands started to work their magic, and she said, "Lift your feet, one at a time." I did. She had planted her foot between mine, and as I lifted each foot, my lower garments were removed completely from my body.

Then, she started on my T-shirt, pulling it over my head.

"We'll be seen," I whispered.

"Well," she replied in a whisper, "you should have worked harder on a tan. Your white body would look like a lighthouse if there was a moon out."

"You should talk," I joked. But her magic was being done. Fully erect, Valerie led me to where she had earlier placed a blanket on the grass. She lay down on her back, pulling me to my knees beside her.

"I wanted to do this outside," she said, "and this seemed to be the perfect night."

Valerie – A Love Story

She pulled me onto her. We held each other. I kissed her passionately, then she spread her legs, and I entered her. The act itself didn't take too long. I squeezed her as I came. I kissed her passionately again, and lay beside her.

I started thinking about being here, in my back yard, completely naked with the twenty-year-old daughter of my neighbor. *If my wife caught us,* I thought, *she'd just doughnut hole us both. That would be ugly. If Valerie's dad caught us, he'd wait until she was clear, shoot me – only shoot me, if I was lucky – and ground her for two months. Jesus! I'm having sex with a woman who still gets grounded as punishment.*

Valerie rolled over, covering half my side with her body. "That was SO wonderful," she said.

"Yes, it was. Despite the fact that I could get shot or sent to jail."

"Nope, not jail," she said. "I'm old enough. Just shot." She giggled.

"You, my love," I said, "are a lunatic."

She rubbed my chest and said, "Don't you know, sex is better with the crazy ones."

I started to laugh, and she 'shushed' me again. Two houses down, a back-porch light came on. I froze. Then, a door opened, I heard the lid of a trash can open and close. The door closed, and the porch light went off.

"You have to learn to relax," Valerie whispered. "You'll have a heart attack if you stress too much. You can't have a heart attack. I want you around a long, long time." There was a pause. We were both enjoying the night. I was thinking about a long, long time – with

Valerie. It was a dream, actually. I didn't think we could possibly have a long, long time together.

She said, "This is so perfect. Completely naked with you. I wonder if this is what it was like in the Garden of Eden."

"Well," I replied, "I don't think there were as many houses, and I don't think Adam was cheating on his wife." I winced as I said the last bit.

"Sort of not true," countered Valerie. "Adam had a first wife. Her name was Lilith. But she wouldn't obey and respect Adam, so God sent her away." I was stunned. I opened my mouth to say something, but before I could even think of anything, Valerie, seemingly lost in thought said, "I'm really glad my parents didn't name me Lilith."

Then, Valerie turned to me and said, "So. She's your first wife."

Before I could reply – not that I had a reply – Valerie was moving on top of me. "One more? Before the night is over?" And we had sex once more. The feel of her against me, her breasts on my chest, her hips moving against mine and me inside her were like magic. I don't know if I made any noise or if she did. It was pure ecstasy.

We were both panting afterward. She hadn't come yet, so I made sure she did. And she was so cute when it happened. Squeezing my hands, her face was angelic. She let out a breath, then lay there for five or ten minutes. We chatted a bit more, then decided we had pushed our luck as far as we could.

"I don't want you to have to sneak back into the house," she said. "I'm so much better at it than you'll ever be. And don't forget that if you ever think about dating another teenager." She giggled again.

"First, this FORMER teenager has just about killed me," I said smiling, "and I wouldn't want any other."

"That's very intelligent of you," she replied.

"But how did you get so good at sneaking," I asked.

She smiled. "To tell you the truth, I think girls are born with it."

She kissed me again, and spread butterfly kisses on my chest and stomach. She said she loved me. Then, she planted a kiss on my manhood. I started to come alive.

"You'll have to take care of that one yourself," she teased. "We've got to get to bed – separate beds." She kissed me again, and put on her robe. She melted into the night. She really was good at sneaking in AND out.

I dressed, picked up her blanket, and headed inside.

The next morning, I noticed something in the back yard. I went out, and saw where the grass was depressed from activities the night before, there were two red roses, with the stems intertwined.

Anna Leigh

Thirty-six

It was September, and as summer had come to an end, the school year started. Valerie decided to leave the community college after just one year and started to attend the women's college she had selected. Her major was international business, but she had a few electives. They wanted to provide a well-rounded education, even for business majors.

It was the season of changes. Valerie called me and said she needed to talk to me. Happily, so I thought, it wasn't *we* need to talk. She wanted to meet me in the next town over from the college. The school was pretty strict about male visitors, and she wanted to avoid any problems with the school. I agreed it would be smarter.

I'd arranged for us to have dinner at a small restaurant and had arrived in town about mid-day. I saw a number of college age women who were being escorted by men. While everything may have been above board, I suspected that this particular town was doing well economically with the assistance of the school policy limiting male contact. Valerie confirmed my suspicions.

"There's kind of an unspoken agreement," she said. "It is like once you enter this town, you go blind.

Nobody ever sees anybody else. Even girls who hate each other never tell. It's weird, but it works."

"I noticed," I said.

"So, I've got a night out – don't ask what I told them."

"Okay."

"I really needed to talk to you, and I figured I might save you the long drive home – as long as you were already here."

"So, what did you want to talk about?" I asked.

"I don't know how to start, so I guess I just will. My mom left my dad."

"Valerie, I'm really sorry . . ." I started to say.

"It is kind of a disaster," she interrupted. "My mom found out my dad was doing more than fantasy football. He was actually betting, a lot of money, on games. And on things other than just games. He lost some money, but when my mom found out and told him she wanted him to stop, he wouldn't do it. She was afraid that if he kept betting more and more money, he'd lose everything they have. So, she made what I guess you would call a preemptive strike. She got a lawyer, froze the assets until a split could be made, and moved into an apartment."

I hugged her and said, "I really am sorry to hear that. Tearing apart a home when there are children – not that you are a child, but it still hurts."

"Well, they were both in their own little worlds. I think my mom was more afraid of losing her ability to socialize. You know, she wants to be able to 'go out,' and she was afraid there wouldn't be anything. This way, she gets half."

"So, what now?" I asked.

"Well, I'm not sure," she answered. "I can't stay with my mom. The place is just too small. I'm not going to go back to 'our' house. My dad will have the place a complete mess, and he will expect me to wait on him hand and foot. Cleaning, grocery shopping, cooking, kitchen duty, laundry. It's not just that it would be – literally – a chore, but I'd never have time for my studies. I obviously can't stay with you, so I'll be staying at school for at least the next month while I sort things out."

I felt for her, and selfishly, I felt for me. Seeing her would be more difficult. "How about money for school?" I asked. "Is that covered, do you need help?" My business was doing okay, although a college education would be a strain.

"No, don't worry. I've got college covered."

"But . . ."

"It's covered," she said.

"How?"

"Would you believe babysitting money?" She had an odd look on her face.

"Valerie, I've never seen you babysit. You're not robbing banks or something, are you?"

She just laughed and said, "You'll understand some day. It IS babysitting money." And she laughed.

Two weeks later, part of her problem was solved, sort of. One of the sophomore girls who was to have gone to study in Paris developed a 'medical issue' that took precedence. I think she developed it in the next town over from the school. Anyway, Valerie was offered the chance to go to Paris for the following semester. While I was happy for her, it meant that she would be farther away, and I would be lucky to see her once or twice. Still, it was her education and she wouldn't have to just sit in the dorm, or run to the next town.

Again, I asked, "Are you going to be able to swing this financially?"

"Yup. And you know how."

I just shook my head in disbelief. I knew she would tell me when she was ready.

The worst news for me was that to avoid having to deal with her mom and dad, she would head to Paris and settle in right after Thanksgiving. I tried to put on a brave face, but it was hard.

"Maybe you could fly to Paris a couple of times. I could send you a ticket."

"Tickets are expensive," I said. "While your 'babysitting money' might help with college, I can't believe it would pay for flights to Paris. And, I'm not going to have you pay for me to come. I'll find a way."

Anna Leigh

Thirty-seven

After our meeting in September, I decided to spend as much time as possible with Valerie before she headed for France, so I made sure that I had weekends free. October arrived, and with it, Valerie's birthday. I hadn't been able to be at her celebration the previous year, so I made sure I would be at this one.

For Valerie's birthday weekend, I made reservations at a small, excellent restaurant that was near her college. I also made reservations at lodge in the college's surreptitious bedroom town – where I'd met Valerie previously. They had bungalows set in a wooded area. Somewhat exclusive, private, and popular. Apparently, lodge owners knew weekend get-aways were important to the ladies at the college.

The bungalow I reserved had a living room, bedroom, and small kitchen. The décor reminded me of a ski lodge. There was a fireplace in the wall between the living room and bedroom. The fireplace opened into both rooms. The floorplan didn't provide much in the way of privacy for those in the bedroom, but since it was only going to be Valerie and me, privacy wouldn't be an issue.

Valerie – A Love Story

I arrived before Valerie. I bought a few snacks, in case they were needed. I also bought flowers and a bottle of champagne. I made sure everything was perfect. Valerie would be heading to Paris soon, and I didn't know when I would see her again. I thought it might be that she would meet someone in France that would sweep her off her feet, and I wouldn't ever see her again. If that was to be, I especially wanted this birthday to be memorable.

Valerie arrived mid-afternoon, on Friday.

"Well," she began, "this is lovely. I'm not sure if I like it better than Santa Barbara, THAT trip was SO special, but this is lovely, and I'm REALLY looking forward to spending my birthday with you. Just try not to get hit by a car." She said it with an impish smile.

I wrapped my arms around her.

"You look sad. Why?" she asked.

"I'm trying not to be, but you have become a very important I my life. I don't know if . . . when we will see each other again."

"Well, first, Silly, we'll find a way to visit once or twice – for the one semester I will be in Paris. And, it won't be as easy to hop over the pond, as they say, as it is to drive up here, it will only be for a few months."

"I know, still." I couldn't see how either she or I would just hop over the pond – the Atlantic Ocean.

"Baby, try not to be sad. We'll have plenty of time – especially after I get back."

I tried to believe. Her energy was infectious, and I found my mood lightening.

Anna Leigh

Dinner was at the restaurant. Of course, I'd picked a French restaurant. But the dinner was exquisite. Valerie's company made it all the more so.

After dinner, we returned to the bungalow. She loved the fireplace, and she was intrigued by having it in the bedroom, as well.

"I've never made love in front of a fireplace. This should be fun."

We started in the living room, but it didn't take long before, after holding each other and sharing passionate kisses, the bedroom seemed to be a better option. So, I picked her up in my arms and carried her to the bed.

"Oh, I'm being ravished!" she said quietly while looking into my eyes.

I set her on the bed carefully, wondering how I was going to make this night special and memorable. Valerie sat up, put her hands around my neck, and pulled me slowly to her. I felt her lips on mine. Her kiss was soft. It didn't last long, but there was no hurry to it, either. She kissed me again, the same way. This time, I felt her lips open and the softness of her tongue played across my lips. I parted my lips to receive her tongue. It was a passionate kiss that seemed to last minutes. It remained soft.

As she kissed me a third time, she reached down and undid my belt, then trousers. She pushed them from my waist, and my erection sprang to life. She gave me a quick kiss on the lips and said, "Well, somebody is glad to see me." Then, she giggled. I found myself thinking, *Valerie will make this night special, like she always does.*

I managed to remove her slacks and briefs while we were enjoying another long kiss. We were both bottomless, but still had tops on. She pulled off my sweater and started unbuttoning my shirt.

"I think I'd like us to be completely naked for this," she said. I removed her top and brassiere.

I pulled back the covers, picked her up, set her where I could cover her, then crawled into bed beside her. We lay holding each other, stroking each other, and kissing.

Valerie looked at the fire and said, "This is like a dream. A beautiful dream. With a beautiful man."

"A troll," I answered, "who doesn't believe he truly deserves to be with the beautiful woman you are."

We kissed again, then, slowly and softly, I entered her. It was the least vigorous sex we'd had. We moved slowly together, enjoying every sensation, captivated by each other's eyes. I felt her chest rising and falling, and her stomach beginning to tighten on mine. When our orgasm came, like the sex, it was soft and prolonged. Still, in the end, we were drained.

"That was incredible," she said. "I didn't know, I mean I never imagined, uh thought, you could just move so slowly and have it be so, so – my God, I don't know what – except it was more than sex, it was spiritual. I . . ."

"You are the one who made it special," I tried to say.

"Well," Valerie smiled, "I think we both had to be there. I mean, I'm only guessing, but I'd say we've both done it alone, and it was never like that."

I started to laugh despite myself. "Yes, I think you may be right. So, you're saying it wasn't you or me? It was US?"

"Yes," she said, "Us."

Thirty-eight

We made love once more that night and again when we awoke in the morning. I was feeling better, but then, I always felt better when I was with Valerie. When I thought back to when I had cleared the walk and drive for the girl who lived next door, I could never have imagined how wonderful she would make me feel and how much she would change my life.

We had a late brunch and enjoyed each other's company for the day. The town was close, but not too close, to Valerie's school. That was the main attraction. There was some shopping, but I had an idea that outdoor activities weren't the main draw for those wanting to visit with their lady friends.

So, getting into the spirit of things, Valerie and I indulged twice more during the day. These were a bit more vigorous – I think we both felt the need to work some of the calories off. We were going to head out to dinner. We were in the shower together. I was having a wonderful time making sure every part of Valerie's anatomy was soaped and rubbed. She was doing the same with me.

"Oh," she said like she'd forgotten something. "I meant to ask you, what if I went off birth control?"

"W-h-a-" I think I got that out after all the air had already left my lungs.

"Oh, are you easy." She laughed. "You know I wouldn't possibly do that without telling you – first. I wanted to see how you would react. I'm going to have to be careful with any practical jokes. I think I stopped your heart just then."

"Of course," she continued, "I would love to have your baby, but right now probably isn't the best time."

"I . . . You . . . What I mean . . ."

By now, she was laughing. "I'm sorry. I didn't realize, well, I didn't think it would be all that."

By then, something else had entered my mind. I was thinking that I would love for Valerie to have my baby. I put my arm around her waist and pulled her tight against me, then, I used my other hand to hold her head while I crushed out lips together. At first surprised, she responded. Her mouth opened and our tongues found each other. I lifted her off the shower floor and managed to place my erection within her. She sucked her breath in as I entered and then let out a long, slow, "Ohhhhh!" I kissed her neck. Her fingers dug into my back. I was aware of her arms tightening around me and mine around her. Just before I came, she looked at me and said, "Why . . ."

I looked into her eyes and said, "I just want you to know how much I actually would love for you to have our baby."

Valerie's legs were around my waist. I felt them tighten, at the same time she squeezed me with her arms. I tightened my arms around her, pressed my mouth to hers, and then, I detonated, coming within her. How I was able to keep standing, I'll never know. Just as my convulsions slowed, Valerie started shaking. Within a minute, we were sitting on the shower floor. Valerie's hands were on my face. She was inches away from me. I heard her saying, "Oh, baby, baby. Baby, I love you so much."

We went to another restaurant that evening. It was lovely – Italian. We tried to eat light, but the Italian food was just too good.

"You look a little pruny," Valerie said. "Like you spent too much time in the water."

"This is what I'll look like in a few decades. Not a pretty sight, is it? By the way, you're looking a bit water-wrinkled yourself. And on you, it looks adorable."

"It's all your fault, you know," she said. "You kept us in the shower too long."

"You started it. You tried to scare the hell out of me – going off birth control. But then, I started thinking how nice it would be if you had our baby."

"Sometime in the future," she said. "But it was a surprise. I wondered if you would get mad or panic. Your reaction, by the way was adorable. But I was really surprised by the second reaction – you know. I'm sorry if I scared you."

We talked about many things after that. I asked about her arrangements for the foreign study program. She said she would be living in Paris – there was a student there with whom she would share an apartment. The other girl would help her get acclimated to the city and everything she would need to know to blend in.

"We'll have to find a way to get you over there – as soon as we can, and as soon as I regain my strength after this weekend."

"I'm sorry," I said. "Do we need to back off?"

"What? No. I'll probably end up crawling back to school, and I won't be able to touch – well, down there, for a week," she smiled broadly as she said it, "but there's no way we're going to slow down this weekend."

We parted on Sunday, during the late afternoon or early evening. We both tried to be upbeat. The drive home was dismal. I didn't want to be there, but for the moment, I had no choice.

Thirty-nine

The time I spent with Valerie in October of her sophomore year was like a breath of fresh air. I felt alive again. Valerie actually left just before Thanksgiving – to avoid having to choose with whom she would spend the day. She said she would want to spend it with me, but that likely wouldn't be possible.

I made sure I was at the airport to see her off. I was tempted to buy a ticket so I could at least be with her on the flight. I knew I was being ridiculous, but it would only have taken a word of encouragement from Valerie and I would have been on the plane. And, in one of the rare instances of my life, I can truly say, money was no object.

After she left for Paris, I missed her terribly. We sent texts, and when we could, we chatted via internet video. But it wasn't the same as sitting next to her, listening to her voice, experiencing her scent. Or, holding her in my arms. Only her presence could provide that, and I couldn't be near her all the time. Then, too, while I wanted what was best for her, I believed she might find someone younger and more interesting in Paris. If not there, then it would likely be somewhere else. I dreaded the day she would find someone else and everything she meant to me would be only a memory.

I had decided, but not discussed with Valerie, that after the holidays, I would move out of the house and start the proceedings for a divorce from my wife. Again, Valerie was the catalyst. I knew that she and I would most likely not have a life – she was young and deserved someone who would be there for her. But I decided that what I was living was not only a deception, it was draining the life from me. I might not have Valerie, but I wouldn't be confined in a loveless prison. I didn't even want to call it a relationship.

I caught up on my projects. As before, Valerie and I had talked about some of the things she was learning in business. As before, I was trying them out. Some of the ideas had worked rather well and had improved my little business. Some didn't, and I discarded those. Some just weren't suited for my particular business model. For her part, Valerie was able to go back to her classes and share what the real-world experiences were with what she had learned. Together, we had improved my efficiency and bottom line. We had also improved her grades, not that they needed much improvement. But 'field testing' theories had made her the teacher's pet, so to speak.

A week later, she called. "I hate to do this," she started. "They've just given up a HUGE project to do, and it is going to keep us busy right up until Christmas. When we – the class – complained about Christmas break, all the professor said was, 'You will still have Christmas Eve and Christmas Day.' I wanted to come back during the break, but there just doesn't look like there will be any time."

She was crying. I might have been, too. "Don't worry about me," I said. "We can make our get-together for after the first. Christmas won't be any fun without you, but I understand. And to be sure you have something from me, I'll send you a small present to open on Christmas."

She was still crying. "It's not fair! I want to be with you. On Christmas – as much as we can be. I know we won't be able to spend all day together – if I were there, but just to see you."

"Well, I want to be with you, too," I answered, "and Christmas is pretty much my one inviolate day, but this will be the one year we won't have." I was hoping we'd have at least one more. "We can be together after the first. I love you."

"I love you, too." Then, still crying, she hung up.

I was hollow inside.

Anna Leigh

Forty

Marsha was home about 7 PM – actually early for her. I wanted to set plans for Thanksgiving and didn't want any last-minute surprises – like some Uncle George visiting from Schenectady.

"So," I began. "What do you want to do for Thanksgiving? We should start getting food together. Do you have any guests you wish to invite?"

Marsha looked at me, as if in thought, then said, "I'm not sure we should do Thanksgiving here this year. I don't have any personal friends I'd invite. Everyone is doing something. Why don't we just make reservations? It seems so silly to spend all day putting together a big meal for a half hour – and for just the two of us."

"But I do most of the work," I countered, "and it's like a day spent preparing for that one big meal. We can do it together. It'll be fun."

"I just don't feel like doing it this year. And besides, I can make reservations that we can change if there are some clients that are interested. And it would be a waste of time for the two of us."

"Clients? Is this about clients?"

"I don't know. It might be. I just want to be prepared."

"And will they be here Christmas morning, as well?"

Marsha just glared at me. I didn't glare, but I stood stone-faced. I couldn't believe she would 'use' the holidays for another sales pitch. She picked up her coat and walked to the door.

"I'll be at the office," she said. "I'll get something to eat downtown."

I was pissed, and frankly, happy to see her go. I wanted to be with, talk with, Valerie, but I couldn't. Being in the empty house was better than being with Marsha.

Anna Leigh

Forty-one

The next couple of weeks passed quietly enough. Marsha and I called a truce, of sorts. We decided, rather she decided, on Thanksgiving dinner at a small relatively exclusive restaurant. It was Thanksgiving, people were eating the traditional meal at home, and they were happy for the business at L'Auberge de Chez Marcel. Whether by design or luck, Marsha did have two people join us. A couple from out of town who were looking for some investment property. It wasn't my idea of Thanksgiving. And I would have thought it would have been far friendlier to have this couple over for a home-style Thanksgiving. But then, maybe Marsha didn't want to have dinner alone with me any more than she wanted to 'waste' a day together with me in the kitchen.

The restaurant was pure class. They tried to do their best with the decorations – Christmas, already. A lot of the decorations were natural, but there were also some plastic things. Just like our celebration.

The couple seemed nice. I tried to be on my best behavior, for their benefit more than for Marsha's. God forbid that I would do something that would 'make' her lose a sale. I'd probably never hear the end of it.

On the ride home – we rode together for a change – she said, "Well, thank you for being civil. I wasn't sure if you would be."

I was having trouble maintaining a positive tone. "No problem. I didn't want to hurt your chances of bringing in your hundredth sale of the year. And, they seemed nice. I don't have any quarrel with them."

"For your information," she replied coldly, "I've closed almost two hundred sales this year."

That was the end of the conversation. When we arrived home, I retired to the couch in my office. The downside was that I could look out my office window and see the window into the dark, empty room where Valerie used to sleep.

Although it was early in the morning in Paris, I sent her a text, 'Just in case you didn't know, ILY."

She must have had her phone on, because within a very short time I received, 'ILY2, Silly."

Anna Leigh

Forty-two

Friday morning, Black Friday in the retail world, was kind of a black Friday all around.

I had made coffee, as I usually did in the morning.

Marsha came into the kitchen and poured herself a cup of coffee. She looked like she hadn't slept – or slept much. "I think you underestimate how much my real estate business means to us and how much money it brings into this household."

I could barely contain myself, but I maintained, as best I could, a calm demeanor. "I appreciate that you are a star in the real estate world," Marsha appeared to brighten a bit, but it wouldn't last. "But I don't believe you understand the toll your *obsession* with being the best of the best has taken and is taking on our marriage." I drew out the word 'obsession,' and avoided saying relationship, because I wasn't sure we even had one anymore.

"If you would be more supportive," she began.

"I've been nothing but supportive," I cut her off. "I've taken care of all the household chores so you could devote your life to this, this business. When you have your soirees, who sets it up, provides the catering, cleaning, waiting, and clean-up afterwards so that you can glide around the room?"

"Well, my business – my career – is important to me. I'm sorry you don't see that."

"More important than me?"

Marsha just stared at me.

"Okay," I started. "I will be moving out, and seeking to end our marriage. I would say relationship, but it hasn't been one for a long time. It will probably be best if I wait until January to leave, but it is over."

"So, you've found someone else?"

I'd already given this a lot of thought. Valerie may have been the catalyst, but I didn't expect she and I would be together forever. Valerie had shown me, however, that life could be better, much better than it was like this.

"I've found," I started, "that we are living like less than roommates. I've found that I no longer want to be in a *relationship* where I am basically treated like the hired help, and someone to take care of the things you don't want to. A relationship where I take second seat to your obsession with this damn business."

"You're going to suffer financially," was her reply.

"This is about much more than money – it is about not regretting my life when I'm lying on my death bed."

"I think you'll find you are wrong," was her comment. She went into the den. I heard her on the phone. I couldn't tell who she had called or what she was saying. When she returned, she said, "I've decided that we don't need to do the holidays" – she said it like the holidays was an abstract concept, not actual celebrations – "this year. I think it best if we can tolerate it, to stay here. After the first, we can see someone to decide how we will split everything up."

While it saved me the trouble of finding a place right away, I wasn't very interested in staying together for the appearance of things.

Forty-three

I called Valerie that evening, late. It was early in the morning in Paris, but I figured she would already be up.

"Good morning, sweet heart," she said in a quiet, not-quite-awake voice.

"Good morning. I wanted to know how you were doing."

"Well, at six in the morning, I'm going to get out of bed and visit the ladies' room, if you must know. But you didn't call just to check on my biologic habits."

"Okay." Busted. "Marsha and I have decided to forego any holiday celebrations this year. In fact, we probably won't be staying together. I wanted you to know."

Valerie was quiet for a moment. I was busy making a mental catastrophe out of her silence.

Finally, she said, "I've got an idea. Why don't you come here for the holidays? My roommate will be out of town, and I understand they have some great celebrations and traditions here."

"I'd love to," I said, "but I need to check finances. And, I might not be able to book a flight – or anything reasonable – at this late date."

We talked for about twenty minutes. She seemed distracted. Then, she said, "Check your in-box. I found a flight to get you here on December 19. The return is for January 1."

I was afraid to see what this might cost. True it would be a free room, but the flights had to be pricey. I opened my e-mail and found what she had sent. British Airways into and out of Heathrow. "This is for London," I said.

"I know," she countered. "Have you ever tried getting in or out of the Paris airport? It is notoriously bad. Besides, with the train, you can get here in no time from London."

"Okay. Okay. Wait a minute! This says the ticket was booked – and paid! How? You can't afford . . ."

"Too late now, Silly," she said. "If I were you, I'd start packing. Oh, yes, you have to put your passport number and other stuff into the site. Just go to 'Manage my booking' enter the ticket number and password – 'Kept man.'" She giggled. "I couldn't resist. Ticket number and last name."

"Look," I started to say.

She shushed me. "I'll explain. But not now."

"I'll see you on December 19. You'd better start packing. Cold weather stuff, too. I wouldn't want you to get cold wearing inadequate winter clothing. And, we can't spend the entire time under the covers." She giggled. We traded 'I love you's' and hung up.

Anna Leigh

Forty-four

I went to the airport on the day of the flight. I had to fly to Washington, DC – well, more correctly, to Virginia – Dulles Airport. The flight to London was on British Airways, and it was scheduled to leave at 10 PM. That meant flying all night, all six hours of it, and landing to meet the sunrise at Heathrow, which is west of London. Then, I had to get to a train station at St. Pancras, wherever that was, to catch the Eurostar to Paris. Valerie had sent me directions.

The flight to Dulles was routine. I collected my bag and headed to the British Airways counter. I stood in line to get my economy seat. When I got to the counter, the woman smiled and told me I was in the wrong place. My face must have dropped a bit. She got someone to take me. It was actually the next counter over. It was called Club World, and I discovered I had a business class ticket. I wasn't sure if you could spank a twenty-one-year-old, but I have to say the thought crossed my mind. I couldn't imagine how much this was costing.

Club World had its own boarding area. The "seats" turned out to be small cubicles with chairs that reclined into small beds. Us Club World-ers were served champagne upon boarding. They greeted me by name. The flight attendants were professional and friendly. Their entire manner was that they really seemed happy that we, as passengers, were there. It was so unlike any domestic US airline I had flown, I couldn't believe it.

The flight left on time. We were served a small but delicious meal, along with wine. Afterward, I reclined my chair into a bed and slept until I was awakened for breakfast before landing. Passport control was easy. Club World gets almost head of the line privileges. When I told the customs agent that I was headed for the Eurostar, I was passed right through. I picked up my bag and headed to the maze that is Heathrow.

Valerie was waiting when I left customs. She was wearing black tight slacks, a red sweater, a white scarf and knit hat, and three-inch heels. I tried not to drool. I asked her why she was meeting me here instead of in Paris, and she just said she didn't want me getting lost. We grabbed a train called the Heathrow Express and headed out, eventually reaching St. Pancras. I called it Saint Pancreas more than once.

As we waited for the Eurostar boarding time, I had to ask, "How did you pay for this ticket? You can't possible afford it. I'm really upset about it. Maybe you deserve a spanking."

"Oooooo," she said with a smile, "sounds like you want to get a little kinky. We could put on some music."

I laughed, then blushed, trying not to think of the picture in my mind. "You know what I mean."

"God," she said, "I'll tell you on the way to France – once we are on the train."

Boarding time finally came. We had to pass through French customs before we boarded. They also x-rayed my bag. Valerie was talking to the attendant in French. I didn't catch everything, but I recognized that she was asking for directions to our coach. Again, I found the coach was designated as Business Class.

Once we were seated, I looked at her and said, "Okay, how?"

"Babysitting money," she giggled.

"You couldn't have afforded this if you had kidnapped the Lindbergh baby and invested the ransom wisely."

"Okay, Silly," she started. Apparently, Silly was her pet name for me. "When I was little, a baby and toddler, my aunt would babysit for me. She loved me very much, and still does. She married a man who became very successful in business. He made A LOT of money, and invested it wisely. They were very much in love, but he was killed in an airplane crash. Aunt Ruth was left with a lot of money – more than enough to take care of her for life. She learned how to invest and she has made the fortune grow."

"That doesn't explain . . ." I started, but she shushed me.

"Aunt Ruth never liked or trusted my biologic father" – as she said biologic she winked and emphasized the word. "So, she set up an account for me. Just her and me. She figured that someday my parents might split up – a smart woman – and she didn't want my father getting any of the money. So, neither my mom nor dad are on the account. Just me and Ruth. She puts more into the account than I can ever use, so college is paid for. And, money for extras.

I stared.

"I said it was babysitting money. I never said I did the babysitting. So, just relax," she continued. "You don't have to meet Ruth until we get to Paris."

I won't say I was panic-stricken. Okay, I was panic-stricken.

"Oh, by the way, the man with whom my Aunt Ruth loved so very much and married was twenty years older than she was. Just saying."

Anna Leigh

Forty-five

We left St. Pancras and made one more stop in England. Just before we entered the Chunnel, as they call it, I saw a huge white horse carved into the hillside. Valerie told me the land was made of chalk and that just carving away the top soil and vegetation exposes the white chalk underneath. The train passed through the tunnel under the English Channel in about twenty minutes. Then, we were in the French countryside. Farmland mostly. It could have been anywhere, but then there would be a village with a church that looked to have been built in the 1600s or 1700s, and I was reminded that I was in an ancient place from where we got a lot of culture and history.

About two hours after leaving London, we arrived at the outskirts of a city, which turned out to be Paris. Sooner than I expected, we were at the station called Gare de Nord. Valerie told me that I should use the toilet on the train; the attended toilettes in the station were very clean, but they cost one euro.

She showed me how to buy a ticket for the Metro. "You have to keep the ticket with you," she said. "If they catch you on the train without one, there is a huge fine.

And," she said with a smile, "if they catch an American on the train without a ticket, they pull out the guillotine."

We descended to the track level. The train came on time. We had to switch trains to get to a stop near her apartment.

She lived in the area next to the Latin Quarter, where her classes were. Valerie told me that it was called the Latin Quarter because in the 'old days' the students and professors there spoke Latin. I was impressed.

The apartment was one floor up. The door had about three locks. Inside, it was comfortable. Cozy, in real estate terms, but roomy enough for her and her roommate. There was a living room, two easy chairs, a couch, and a coffee table. Hardwood floors and a rug covering most of the floor. There was a small kitchen. Two bedrooms and a bathroom finished out the floor plan. A window overlooked the street below.

"I don't like to have anyone bother my roommate's stuff," she started with a smile, "so I guess you'll have to bunk in with me."

I was going to try to play it cool, but I grabbed her and kissed her, wrapping my arms around her tightly. My heart was pounding. It felt so incredibly great to have her near.

She kissed me back – then said, "You'll bunk in with me, but first, we need to go to dinner."

"Why?" I asked.

"Because you have to meet Aunt Ruth," she said.

Okay, I was back in panic-stricken mode.

Forty-six

The restaurant was lovely. I couldn't judge how expensive it was. Even in some small cafés in Paris, the waiters dress formally, so there was no clue there. Valerie and I were ushered to a booth across an aisle from the window. A woman was already seated. She appeared to be slightly older than me, although I couldn't tell how much older. She had the look of someone who exercised and took care of herself.

"Aunt Ruth," Valerie started, "I'd like to introduce Jim Conner. Mr. Conner, this is my Aunt Ruth." A formal introduction caused alarm bells to sound somewhere in my brain.

"It is a pleasure to meet you," I said, shaking her hand.

"Oh, come now, Valerie," Ruth said. "You'll scare the hell out of poor Mr. Conner." She held out her hand again and said, "Ruth."

I took it and said, "Jim."

"Now that that is done," Ruth said, "how about some food. I'm starved."

Dinner was lovely. The weather was cold. We had onion soup, quiche Lorraine, and salad. Ruth chose a local red wine, which was delicious.

The talk was light and I was starting to feel at ease. Valerie excused herself to visit the ladies' room. Ruth remained at the table. When Valerie was gone, Ruth reached over and put her hand on my forearm. "This has been a very lovely evening. I'd love to talk some more. Why don't you meet me at the Café La Petite Souris tomorrow – about noon – just us two. We can chat." My ease left and my panic returned.

Valerie and I parted company with Ruth after dinner. On the walk back to the apartment, I told Valerie that Ruth wanted to meet me at noon the next day. She seemed unaffected and brushed it off. "You two will have a nice talk, I'm sure."

I wasn't sure, and although we made love, and I was exhausted from travel, I didn't sleep.

Anna Leigh

Forty-seven

Café La Petite Souris was a small, almost intimate restaurant on a quiet street not far from Valerie's apartment. I wore a pair of dress slacks, dress shirt, sweater, and slip-on shoes. I wanted to look nice, but didn't want to give away how nervous I felt.

Ruth was seated at an outside table. She was wearing black slacks and a black sweater. She had what looked like a wide scarf in a dark brown and black pattern. She had it around her neck; it draped below her waist both in front and back. A black beret and black three-inch heels completed her ensemble. Outside heaters kept the temperature warm enough for outside dining, although I think Parisians would dine out in the cold, anyway.

"Jim," she said, "how nice of you to come."

"It is my pleasure, Ruth," I said, taking a cue from her. *How nice of me to come,* I thought, *how could I refuse? Lord knows, I wanted to. Refuse, that is.*

It was a small table with the chairs on either side, both chairs facing the sidewalk, which was two tables and ten feet away.

"Valerie has told me quite a bit about you," she began. "She doesn't have many friends she trusts with *important* information. She calls me from time to time."

I was at a loss. I'd only known about Ruth for two days.

"She actually called me after she said she ambushed you with a kiss. She said she had fallen in love."

"I remember the ambush," I said – lamely.

"You seem nervous, off balance," she continued. "Not to worry. You've only known about me for two days, well, not quite two full days. I've known about you for more than a year. Wine?" She looked at the waiter approaching. She ordered something in French. In a few minutes, the waiter returned with a bottle of red wine, two glasses, and a plate with cheese and bread.

"Don't worry," she continued, "I'm not going to try to ply you with wine and extract information."

"I," was about all I got out.

"Because I already know a great deal about you," she continued. I choked on a sip of wine.

"You okay?" she asked, looking at me.

"Anyway," she continued, "Valerie means more to me than you will ever know."

"Me, as well," I said.

"Yes, I'm sure. Of course, I've set up a fund for Valerie. I understand she has told you about this?"

"Yes, just yesterday. She kept buying things she couldn't afford, at least I didn't think she could afford them, and I was worried about how she was doing it. She told me it was 'babysitting money.'"

"Babysitting money?" Ruth asked.

"Yes. She explained yesterday that she got it as a result of you babysitting her. And here I was, thinking she was babysitting for some ultra-rich couple, or just trying to tell me not to worry."

Ruth laughed. "But you do worry about her, don't you?" Ruth asked.

"Yes, I do. I love her," I looked at Ruth as I said it, "and I don't want anything bad to happen to her – ever. I want the best for her."

"As do I," said Ruth. "What if – what if the best for her didn't include you?" she asked.

I felt a giant's hand crush my heart at the thought. "If I really thought the best thing for Valerie didn't include me, I would miss her very, very much. And I will admit – maybe you are plying me with wine – there are days when I don't think I deserve her." I hated to say it, but it was the truth.

"Well," said Ruth, taking a sip of wine, "it isn't every day that a man will jump in front of a car for a woman."

"I didn't really intend to jump in front of the car," I said. "I just needed Valerie not to be in front of it, and that was the only thing I could do at the time. The only thing that mattered was to save her."

"You seem very nice," she said. "I like you. It would seem that what we have in common is Valerie's welfare – no matter what it costs us. A toast – to Valerie?"

Valerie – A Love Story

    I wasn't sure just what the hell the last meant, but I toasted to Valerie. We finished the wine and I headed back to Valerie's apartment, feeling a bit uneasy, but wanting to see Valerie more than ever.

Anna Leigh

Forty-eight

That afternoon, feeling a bit dizzy from the wine, Valerie and I boarded a train and headed to Innsbruck, Austria. She had always wanted to see it, and she said the shopping would be good. The train took just about eight hours to reach Innsbruck, which sits in the Austrian mountains. The scenery was breathtaking. The shopping was nice, but just being there with Valerie was enough for me. After her birthday weekend, I considered any time I could spend with her to be a bonus.

I kept thinking about my lunch earlier in the day. After my conversation with Valerie's aunt, I wasn't sure what the future held, her words were cryptic, and I wasn't sure I even wanted to know what they might have meant. I wanted to spend every moment I could with Valerie. I knew I was almost obsessed, but I couldn't be with her enough. I hoped I wasn't smothering her.

We stayed the night in a small bed and breakfast. We made love, and afterward she told me that she loved being with me, and that I made her feel so very special. In the morning, we had breakfast, then headed back to Paris. In Paris, we went to the Louvre, the Tuileries, and went shopping. She insisted on doing some shopping separately, so we could buy Christmas presents for each other that would be 'secret' until Christmas. We actually agreed to buy two presents each – one for Christmas Eve, and one for Christmas morning. The next two days were spent enjoying the pre-Christmas spirit and events in one of the most beautiful cities of the world.

On Christmas Eve, we attended a concert of carols, sung in French. The concert was held in a small chapel, built in the 1600s. Heated by small fireplaces, the building was cold, but we expected that, and it only made us huddle closer, if that was even possible. The weather was cold, and despite our nuzzling as close as we could, we were both freezing by the time we got back to Valerie's apartment.

We had purchased a small tree and decorated it. We put the last of the decorations on it that evening. We exchanged Christmas Eve gifts. She had gotten me a beautiful pen, and I had gotten her an antique brooch. She said she was thrilled, and threw her arms around my neck. I put my arms around her. Soon, we were kissing and we didn't even wait to get to her room before our clothes were scattered and we were making love.

Christmas morning, we were up with the sun. Valerie had invited her aunt for dinner, but before we cooked dinner, we had to straighten the place up from our debauchery the night before. We exchanged our Christmas gifts. Valerie had gotten me a beautiful watch, I told her she had spent too much. I bought for her a tennis bracelet, which she loved but said it broke our spending agreement. I told her that when you factor in the cost of the flight over – it got me nowhere. But it wasn't a serious argument, anyway. That was the funny thing. Even when we disagreed, Valerie and I were able to discuss it calmly. I couldn't imagine what an argument would be like, except, of course, I would lose.

We roasted a small turkey and made the traditional American Christmas dinner. It might not have been completely appropriate in Paris, but we thought we were combining the best of two worlds. Valerie's aunt arrived about a half hour before dinner. We had drinks and she presented us with small gifts. She complimented us on our cooking – saying Valerie could learn something from me – stayed a short time after we ate, then excused herself.

The next week together went quickly. Valerie had some things she had to finish for the new term, and I spent my time reading or ogling Valerie.

New Year's Eve, as always was happy and sad. The old year was a very good one. I was sad to see it go. And while the coming year might bring good things, it was likely going to be a difficult journey.

I said goodbye to Valerie at Gare du Nord. I told her I wouldn't get lost, and even if I did, it wasn't important. I was only going back to the States, I avoided using the term 'home.' I wasn't sure I even wanted to be there.

The flight on BA was as good as the one on the way to Valerie. It just wasn't as much fun or filled with as much anticipation. Something about her aunt's words haunted me. While I tried not to think about what that might be, I had a feeling of unease.

The flight landed in the U. S. on time. Customs took a little while, then I was on another airplane, on my way back home. Whatever 'home' meant.

Valerie – A Love Story

A note in my office read, "We have an appointment on January 28th to start splitting everything up." As usual, even though I knew who it was from, it wasn't signed. I guess I wasn't worth it. But it didn't matter. Painful as it might be, Marsha wasn't my future, even if Valerie might not be either. Still, I felt alone.

Anna Leigh

Forty-nine

Thursday morning, ten days after New Year's I was in my office, asleep. I'd started sleeping there after my row with Marsha. It was about 5 AM, and I dreamed I was back in the Navy, in the engine room of a ship at sea, with the engine making this pounding sound. I wondered why I was on the ship, then, the pounding stopped and started again. Slowly waking, I realized that there was someone at the door.

I tried to pull myself out of sleep and bed. I wondered whether someone had the wrong house, maybe a drunk. But then I figured all the drunks were either sober at 5, or home, passed out. I also gave passing thought that Valerie's father had finally found out who his little girl had been seeing, and he was here to extract his revenge. Walking past the bedroom, I noted that Marsha was not in bed.

I pulled on a robe and wobbled down the stairs. The pounding stopped when I yelled, "I'm coming. I'm coming."

I opened the door to find two state troopers standing on the porch. I remember thinking that for 5 AM, their uniforms looked unbelievably perfect. Then, I realized that Marsha, out at one of her evening dinner meetings, must have had too much to drink and been arrested for DUI. It wouldn't do her reputation any good.

"Good morning, trooper." I decided to keep it professional. "How may I help you?"

"Are you Mr. James Conner?"

"Yes, Sir."

"And your wife is Marsha Conner?"

"Yes, sir. May I ask what she has done?"

"Well, sir," he started. "There isn't any good way to say this. I have some bad news. Your wife was in an accident last night." He paused.

"Is she all right?" I was suddenly concerned.

"I'm afraid she ran a red light and her vehicle was hit by another vehicle. She and the male passenger in her vehicle did not survive. It was quick, and neither of them suffered."

My legs were weak. My vision became fuzzy. I couldn't really hear what the trooper was saying. The words were muffled and I could hear a pounding inside my head.

I think they asked if they could come in. They helped me to the couch. I sat staring at the floor.

"We will need you to come down to the morgue and make a positive identification. I know this is difficult, but it is something we need to do – the sooner the better."

Anna Leigh

I don't know how long I sat on the couch, staring. I don't know if I said anything or asked any questions. They were patient.

"We need to . . ." I started, then paused.

"We need to have you identify your wife," said the trooper.

I wasn't sure what to do. "Do I need to shave? Wear a coat and tie?" I had no idea what the protocol was or if there was one.

"You can dress casually, sir," said the second trooper.

I went upstairs, shaved and showered as quickly as I could, and put on my best slacks, shirt, and shoes. I put on a sport coat, but no tie. I couldn't breathe with one. The troopers drove me to the morgue. I don't think I was coherent enough that they trusted me to drive myself. I don't remember the ride.

As expected, neither the exterior nor interior were very cheerful. I dreaded entering the building and wondered how people worked in such a dismal place. There was an antiseptic odor as soon as I walked in the door. The walls were covered with sickly green tiles. There were a few preliminaries. I had to produce identification. Then, all too soon, I was ushered into a room. There was the form of a body under a sheet. I remember thinking that the room was too cold for anyone just covered with a sheet.

When she was much younger and more adventurous, my wife had gotten a tattoo. It was a small bird on her left hip – a place where she could display it when she wanted, but hide it when she wished to appear more 'proper.' I told them about the tattoo. A man in a long white lab coat checked and lifted the sheet just far enough for me to see the tattoo. It was hers. Her naked form was on the gurney, covered with a sheet only. Square doors in the background covered the cold storage into which she would be put. I found myself thinking, *what would she think if she knew she would be put on display like this?* I brought myself back to reality.

I vomited.

Someone asked if I was okay. I wasn't, but I nodded anyway.

The coroner lifted the sheet far enough for me to see most of my wife's face. Not all of it was visible. I started as if to lift the sheet further, but I was stopped. A voice said, "Your wife suffered significant damage there in the crash. It would be best if you didn't look." I didn't.

"Is this your wife?" someone asked. I nodded.

"I'm sorry but we need an oral affirmation," the same voice said.

"Yes. That is my wife."

The sheet was replaced and I was led out of the room. I signed a paper saying I was who I said I was and testifying that the body was that of my wife. Then, I was driven home.

Over the next day or so, the police interviewed me to determine what I knew about the night she was killed. And, I found out that after a successful sales dinner, she closed a big account. After the dinner, she and the young man, Bill, who was her assistant that night, had gone somewhere for a celebratory drink. The only problem was that the accident had happened at 4 AM, long after any bars had closed. Then, it came out that both had engaged in sexual intercourse sometime shortly before the accident. I didn't know how I felt.

It also came out that when she ran the red light, her vehicle was hit broadside by a tractor-trailer that had the right of way, doing about 60 miles per hour. I doubt they even knew what hit them.

Fifty

The funeral was three days later. I guess she was well thought of, or at least well known. There were about a hundred people in attendance. All of her co-workers expressed their sympathies for my loss and told me how important she was for the business. I didn't tell anyone that it was the business that I thought drove us apart and that I was moving out shortly.

A tall blonde was one of the last to approach me. She was dressed nicely, but a bit more seductively than I would have expected: skirt hem well above the knee and a bit too much cleavage showing.

"It is just such a shame that she died so young. You must miss her terribly."

"Yes," I said, continuing the charade. The truth was, I felt badly about her passing, even guilty.

"Of course," the blonde continued, "rumor has it – not that I believe in rumors – that she and Bill were out later than they needed to be, and . . ."

"Yes," I cut her off, "I've heard the rumors. Frankly, I think the fact they were killed is by far the most important thing here, no matter what else happened, two people are dead. AND, spouting rumors at a funeral service for them is in incredibly bad taste."

She looked like she had been slapped and left in a huff. I was wondering how bad humanity had gotten to be.

I headed home to an empty house. Over the years, I had gotten used to being in an empty house. Now, it seemed even emptier, somehow.

Fifty-one

Two days later, I got a call from her office – former office. They needed me to come in and sign some papers. I made an appointment for noon, although they said it wouldn't matter. They would see me anytime I arrived.

I arrived just before noon and was greeted by a tearful receptionist. She told me that my wife was really a nice person and that she couldn't believe such a terrible thing had happened to her. I thanked her for her kind words and told her I hoped she would feel better soon. I was taken to the office of the acting head of the agency, Jennifer Long.

"Mr. Conner," she began, "I wish we were meeting under better circumstances. This has been a great shock to all of us here, just as I'm sure it was to you." Her phrasing and tone seemed prepared, although sincere. "Your wife's things are being packed and we will deliver them to you in a day or two." Her voice began to sound hollow. "I hope that is acceptable."

"We have a few things for you to sign, if you would please." The things they wanted me to sign were two insurance policies. The first was a keyperson policy, common to insure the primary leader of a company, it provides funds to help keep the company solvent during the loss transition. Why I had to sign that, I didn't know. Ms. Long said the attorneys wanted it signed. It didn't matter to me. The second was a surprise. It was a second insurance policy, with me as the benefactor, and the amount was significant. Very significant.

"The second policy was taken out by your wife," she paused, "in the event something like this happened. Instead of buying out her share of the business, the business transfers to the," she paused again, "surviving officers. The policy pays you what would have gotten from the sale of her interest. Our attorneys will help shepherd this through the insurance company," she continued. "Sometimes, with a policy of this size, they tend to delay paying as long as possible. One other thing," she looked a little worried, "we would like to ask that you sign a release stating that you hold the company harmless."

"What? Why?"

Jennifer looked a little frightened. "Well, your wife was killed as a result of her own actions, but some might argue that she was on company business. We would hope to avoid any litigation against the company for her death. We think that any litigation would be expensive for everyone and get us – you and the company – nowhere. And, it could bankrupt the company and put all of these people out of work."

"Jennifer," I said, "I don't have any problem signing something like that – as long as there is also a clause that holds me and my wife's estate harmless, as well, and that any litigation on the part of the truck driver or the driver's company are handled and paid by this company."

She seemed greatly relieved. Her attorney had the document drown up in short order. Just to be sure, I had it reviewed by legal counsel before I signed it, as well. *You only need an attorney to protect you against other attorneys.*

Anna Leigh

Fifty-two

The office door still read, David Anderson, PhD – Clinical Psychology. It was late January, and I was trying to absolve myself of the guilt I felt over the death of my wife.

"So, Jim," he started, "we began last time and didn't get very far. Why don't you start wherever you wish?"

"Like I said last time, my wife was out late at night, celebrating after closing a big deal. She was drunk, and possibly distracted, ran a red light at the worst possible time, and got herself - and a man she was with – killed."

"And you feel guilty?

"Yes."

"Were you supposed to be along with her that night?"

"No."

"Did you know she was going to drink after dinner?"

"No."

Valerie – A Love Story

"Who was the man she was with?" he asked, changing slightly his approach.

"He was a young man from her office, sent along to help her carry papers, that sort of thing."

"And who chose him to go along?"

"I guess my wife did."

"So, if you didn't make you wife attend this dinner, didn't make her go out afterward and didn't choose who went with her, why is it you feel guilty?"

"Probably because I have been seeing someone outside of our marriage." I left out the part about how old she was when we started our relationship and just who she was, just as I had when we first met, when I was trying to decide to leave my wife.

"So, did this third party," I noticed his avoidance of the term 'other woman' "make your wife attend this dinner, make her go out afterward or choose who went with her."

"No," I said. "She is currently out of the country and doesn't even know my wife was killed."

"You haven't told her?"

"No."

"Why not?"

"I'm conflicted."

"About?"

"What do you mean, 'about?' I've been seeing another woman. I was going to separate from my wife after the new year, now she's dead – a result of a violent crash — and I'm financially very well off because of it. While I was planning to leave my wife, the other woman — which you avoided calling her — was the catalyst. I never thought she and I would be together."

"So, you were hoping your wife would find out about her and make the whole job easier on you?"

"No. I truly care for this woman, and love being with her. There are just reasons I didn't think we would be together. I thought she would eventually end up with someone else."

"Is she married? Did she agree to be your co-respondent?"

"No. Neither."

"I would like to know more about this mysterious woman who you claim to love, and I assume loves you, but yet — even though not married — you don't expect to be with in the distant future. There is something there you aren't telling me."

"Yes," I said, "there are things I'm not telling you, but I don't' think it is important for our purpose."

"This woman is integral to our purpose. She is the reason you feel guilty for your wife's death. Whether you are important to her, I don't know. I do know that she is and has been the most important thing in your life for some time."

Even though that might all be true, I couldn't divulge who she was and just how young she was when we started.

Fifty-three

I went through this process with the psychologist for some time. I didn't think it was getting me anywhere. I also decided to seek the spiritual counselling of a minister – though I haven't been to church in ages. I picked a small, old Catholic church in another town.

"Thank you for seeing me, Father." A priest. I guessed his age to be somewhere in his eighth decade. He was alert and looked to be energetic. His hair was medium length, neat, and gray. His eyes were blue, and looked like they held the wisdom of the ages. But his eyes also looked like he had seen a great deal in his life, and much of that wasn't good.

"I'm not sure of the purpose of our meeting, my son," he started.

"I need your opinion, Father – your thoughts. Before we start, however," I handed him an envelope with a large donation to his church.

"Thank you, my son. Your problem must be a weighty one. But, I'm not sure I can help."

"It doesn't matter. I'm not looking for absolution. I just need your thoughts. Like the character in 'Dante's

Inferno,' I have awoken to find myself in a dark wood. I need the insight of a spiritual man to help me." I went through the information I had given the psychologist, again, leaving out the specifics of the who and age of Valerie.

"First, I can't absolve you of anything you have done. An intimate relationship outside the marriage contract is something I cannot approve. And even if I did say you are absolved, you wouldn't accept that. You seek absolution for something that does not require absolution."

"I'm not seeking absolution; just perspective with which I can know my motivation and learn to live with what I may have been responsible for."

We talked for a half hour or so. Then, he said, "So. Let me ask you these questions. I don't expect you to answer them all for me, but in the future, I hope you will be able answer them for yourself. Let's start with the easy ones."

"First, did you make your wife have a dinner with clients or drink afterward?"

"No," I answered.

"Second, did you have any part in your wife's running the red light?"

"No," I answered.

"Those were easy. More difficult, 'Did you contribute to the deterioration of your marriage? Did you make your wife bury herself in her business?" I was quiet.

"Now, did your wife cause you to look outside your marriage for companionship? Did you attempt to engage your wife when you saw you were attracted to someone else – as the alternative?"

"If your wife is not responsible for what you did, and you seem to take responsibility for that yourself, then you cannot take responsibility for the things she did – that ultimately led to her death."

"Why do I feel guilty? Can you tell me that?"

"You wished to resolve that conflict. When your wife was killed, and if I may be direct, you have essentially profited by her death. I think you may feel guilty because you've paid no penalty for what wrong you may have done or felt you've done, and your wife has paid a great penalty for something that came between you, but may not be wrong in the ethical sense. It is like cheating in a game and winning. You don't feel it is honorable. And yet, this isn't a game. It is in conflict with who you think you are."

"How do I – how do I resolve this?" I asked.

"Life is gray. It is not black and white. Of course, if people did not stray, there would be no need for clergy. Your job is to do the best you can – that is rarely perfection, which you appear to believe you need to achieve. Go home. Walk. Think. Feel. Try to forgive yourself."

"I think much of your guilt comes from the fact that in a way, you feel relieved that she is out of your life, and deep down inside the fact that you are relieved by her death is destroying your soul."

"So, what do I do?"

Anna Leigh

"If you were one of my parishioners, I'd have you say one hundred rosaries, and let God into your heart to prove that not everything is controlled by us."

"And people who are not your parishioners?"

"Why do you ask?"

"To put it the best way I can, because my soul needs it."

"Then, do this, my son. Once a week, go to a church. Light a candle. Sit for a few minutes. Think about how we are not in control of the universe and all the things that happen. If you wish, ask forgiveness for those things you believe you have done wrong. But remember also, we are all human. God didn't make us perfect."

"Also, think about this," he continued. "If you could not control the events of the night your wife was killed, who did? Maybe it was all part of God's plan after all. None of us can truly understand why things happen, but we don't control them."

"Are you saying that God," I didn't know how to say it, "God was responsible for my wife's death?"

"When you read the Bible, my son, you will find that God is credited with many things. – many that seem contrary and don't make sense to us now. You must walk by faith, not by sight."

So, I went to church and lit a candle. And sat. And thought.

I went home. I walked. I thought. I felt. I also went through the things from Marsha's office, and the things she had in our, now my, home. Much was donated or thrown. It may have been soon, but I was planning on selling the house and moving. Where, I wasn't sure.

I came to realize that I was responsible for what I did, and Marsha was responsible for her actions even though they caused her death. I might have been wrong in my relationship with Valerie, but I had tried to revitalize my marriage. The revitalization hadn't worked. Marsha had turned me down – repeatedly – when I tried to do things to get closer – even before Valerie. In the end, I was comfortable with shared responsibility, and shared forgiveness. I still felt guilty that Marsha's death had enriched me financially. After two months, the priest was right. While I didn't feel good about it, I had come to grips with why I felt guilty.

In March, I flew to Paris.

Anna Leigh

Fifty-four

"You didn't tell me!?" Valerie was incredulous. I couldn't blame her.

"Please," I said. "I know. I was wrong. But first there was the shock. Then, I just didn't know what to say. I didn't want to screw up your work here."

"Stop right there," she said. "My work is never, and will never be as important as supporting you and being there for you when you need me."

"I'm truly sorry, but I needed to sort myself out before I could be any good for you. I love you, but I didn't want to think I was saying, 'Well my wife is gone and now everything is open for us.' You deserve the best, and I love you more than I can ever say, but – and I'm afraid, really, to say this – I'm afraid I'm not the 'best' you deserve."

"Stop that right NOW!" she almost screamed. "I will decide who is the best for me and who I deserve. And I never want to hear you say that or anything like that again! Got it? You jumped in front of a car for me!"

"To be honest, I pushed you from in front of a car. I was just stupid enough not to get out of the way myself."

She wasn't in the mood for quips. Even if what I was saying was true.

We talked at length. I told her what I had gone through. I told her how hard it was to identify Marsha's body. She might not have liked that, but I also said that even though I was going to move out after the holidays, having her die in that way was still emotionally destructive. As we talked, she seemed to understand, although she said she still didn't forgive me for not telling her when I would have needed her most. And yet, she seemed distant – distracted.

"I wanted to be strong and not have you think I couldn't handle it – even though you would have made it much easier. And I didn't want to burden you."

We walked through Paris. We didn't have sex. She said I had picked her 'time of the month' to visit, and she said she didn't feel comfortable having sex during that time. We spent our days cuddling and enjoying each other's company. But she still seemed distracted, pensive.

Two days before I was scheduled to return to the U.S., Valerie was having coffee in the morning. She was wearing pajamas and still looked great. But she just about stopped my heart.

"There is something I need to tell you," she said.

I panicked. This statement is only second in producing terror behind the infamous, 'We need to talk.' I braced myself, but not enough.

"Okay," I said.

Valerie looked very serious. "I'm getting married – in about a year."

Anna Leigh

Fifty-five

I don't really know what I did. For the second time in three months, I had received news that made my legs weak and my vision fade. If I would have fainted, it wouldn't have surprised me. I waited WAY too long before responding. While I knew this was coming someday, I never wanted it to be today.

"I'm very happy for you. I hope you will be very happy."

She said, "I don't think you sound very happy."

"I was just caught by surprise." It was the truth, and a lie. I felt like my life was ending, but it had been inevitable. A giant had his hand around my heart and was squeezing. I wanted to die. Finally, I realized I needed to say something.

"So, can I ask who the lucky man is?"

"Oh, GOD!" she said. "It's YOU! You're the lucky man. God, I'm going to have to be SO careful with you. You are SO sensitive. If I hadn't told you it was you, you might have jumped off a building or done something else incredibly stupid."

I think my heart skipped a beat. This time for joy, but it couldn't be. "Val," was all I got out.

Valerie started, "Don't start with that 'we are so different in age,' and all that stuff. We have had a great relationship so far, and I want that for the rest of my life. You've done nothing but help me, respect me, and if I can believe you, love me."

"I do love you," I interjected.

"You saved my life. Maybe I shouldn't tell you this, but I've wanted you for as long as I can remember. Our relationship is based on love and respect and sharing and wanting to be together and travelling through life together. *Obviously*, I'm going to have to take charge of this relationship."

"I, you, what?"

"Okay. Let's review. You needed a push with my peach iced tea. You needed a push when I rubbed against you at your party. Doing the striptease dance scared the hell out of me, but you liked it, and I knew I was right. Well, maybe not right then, but later. Then, I attacked you a couple of times. So, I've shown I know what is best for you. Care to tell me I'm wrong? You better not. And, we're getting married next year. You and me. I love you."

I was speechless. I'd been steamrolled. And, I had to admit, I loved it – well the outcome. Not so much the beginning when I saw my life coming to an end. But I told her that because I was an older, and married, man, I didn't feel I had the right to impose on her. It was going to be up to her what we might do and when we might do it. "Even after," I paused, "I was no longer married, I didn't feel I could just say – again – okay, I'm now ready. You might not have wanted to continue – long term."

"I'll show you long term, buster," she said it in a playful way. "I'll still be around when we are both dust bunnies."

Fifty-six

Valerie and I didn't marry the following year. We married about six months later. In a small chapel near Paris. It was September, and autumn was particularly spectacular that year. The leaves stayed on the trees, and the reds, yellows, and oranges were vibrant. Valerie's gown was a pale blue. It was a very small ceremony. Her aunt arrived for it. I was pleased to see her. She told me that Valerie had spoken of me often, and while she had cautioned Valerie about becoming involved with an older married man, Valerie's descriptions of our relationship had softened her concerns. And now, she was glad the man who had made Ruth's treasure so happy would be with her. Frank Shields flew in from the West Coast of California. I was glad to see him and made him my best man. Ruth was Valerie's maid of honor. When she asked me what I wanted for our wedding dinner, I said, "Cake."

Valerie finished her requirements early and earned a month of time off until the next term started. We spent two weeks touring Paris and two weeks in the French, Swiss, and Italian Alps. Valerie found a way to get her university work done and spend time with me, as well.

Anna Leigh

I had returned to the States after Valerie announced we were going to marry. I put the house up for sale – with Marsha's old firm. They actually had it sold in a short time. Some of the single women at her firm, sensing that I would soon be "on the market," started making overtures – "It must be very hard now." "If you need anyone to talk to . . ." "You look like you are losing weight – why don't we go to dinner?" It was almost funny. I couldn't wait to get back to Paris.

When she wasn't studying, Valerie and I toured the Louvre, saw the sights of Paris, and enjoyed the cuisine in the absolute best place on earth to eat. We also continued to wear ourselves out physically.

Valerie talked about combining her acquired knowledge in business with art, opening a shop to cater to those looking to buy quality paintings, sculpture, etc. It sounded like a good idea. She arranged to complete her studies in Paris instead of returning to the women's college "up the road" from where we used to live.

My French was atrocious, but Valerie said that if I studied hard and improved, there would be a "special reward." There was, and my French improved – significantly.

Another of her ventures turned out to be a real money maker. It seems she showed her twenty-page paper about Medieval Sadie and Sophie to one of her professors. He suggested that she do a bit more research and make it longer and more comprehensive. It is now a little book that high schools buy for their advanced placement history courses, and at least one college in every state requires it in their world history 101 courses.

Valerie – A Love Story

We split our time between Europe and the United States. We have a home in the US not far from where we met, although it is in a more rural area. It is now some years later – the number doesn't matter. We have been married for; we'll just say somewhat more than two decades. We have two wonderful children, a boy and a girl, now both in college in the states. They care for the home we have there. We continue to spend most of our time in France, near Paris. Valerie is as beautiful as ever, probably more so. With everything she has accomplished, she has made me the number one priority in her life. I cannot believe I have been so blessed.

This part of my life is like a completely different lifetime. When I look back, I am sorry for some of the things that happened, but I realize that what came out of that time when I wasn't happy, when I was stuck in a situation neither good nor bad, I know that I made the right choice – or maybe Valerie made it for me. I am glad, either way. Had I known how wonderful my life would turn out, I would have started this story, "Once upon a time, . . ."

7/17

Made in the USA
Middletown, DE
28 July 2019